Where the heart belongs

Scarlett Heir

Contents

Chapter-1: Pilot.

M^{AIRA}

"What a stunning performance it was!!" were the host's words through the speakers.

Apparently it was our fresher's party going on, different performances and speeches were happening.

This was the first occasion after I had decided to put on a niqab. So basically I was the odd one out here. Some would just give me a single weird glance and some would keep staring at me till I feel extremely awkward. But I was already prepared, I knew all the consequences which would come with this.

Our seniors were the main in-charge of this event. Two of them were hosting on the Dias and four to five of them were managing the other things off stage.

But a certain guy caught my attention. He had this thick yet silky black hair, a five 'o' clock shadow on his surprisingly sharp jawline and a perfect pair of eyes whose color was not much visible, probably due to the set of vintage glasses which he had put on.

He would clench his jaws every now and then while raking fingers through his hair. He had put on a black jacket with red piping on it. The jacket was unbuttoned and every time he would lift his hands, the black shirt would peep through.

And I was shamelessly checking him out!

Astaghfirullah.

I instantly did istaghfar for the act which I myself didn't know why I was doing.

I had done my best at lowering my gaze from the beginning of this year in this college, until now.

I cannot believe I even saw the color of the shirt he was wearing beneath his jacket.

Astaghfirullah again!

Throughout the whole event I tried my best to not look at his side.

"Tried" being the keyword.

Finally it was all over. My home was a five minutes walk away from the university. Returning back home was the most relaxing thing that happened in the whole day. Mama was in her room, giving her a quick Salam I made my way to my room.

Home is usually like this when I return back. My elder brother, Usman comes at nine in the night. Baba would be back in about an hour now. And then all of us together would have dinner and retire to bed.

This is my family, the most loving and caring parents and an annoying yet awesome big brother. Protective might I add.

I drift off to sleep with a certain black jacket guy's face on my mind.

Ya Allah, help me.

(◍•ᴗ•◍)

University was good, exams were not coming any sooner. But Mr. Cooper who was currently trying to explain mathematics was taking this more seriously than us.

A senior from the next class came in suddenly and started talking to Mr.Cooper, good that we got a break from his lecture.

"Miss. Maira Abdul Haseeb, who is it here?" he asks suddenly.

"It's me, sir."

"Mrs.Henley has asked for you. Go with her."

"Uh OK sir." I was surely blank about the whole thing.

I mentally go through all the things which would lead me to detention or any other trouble.

"Would you do me a favour Maira?" Mrs.Henley asks as soon as I entered her office.

"There's going to be a workshop this Saturday, would you be able to do a speech on that day?"

"Yeah sure. If you give me the required details." She didn't really give me a choice in asking a favour though, so there was no use of any further discussions.

There were two people whom I somewhat grown close to in this time here in university, Amina and Zainab. My two other best friends were in different places, Alina and Maryam. We have sleepovers in a month or two and fill the void of not being together all the time.

Now coming back to the class I told Amina and Zainab about the workshop and the speech I had to give.

(▥•ᴗ•▥)

"I am taking your laptop for tomorrow alright?" Well that's my brother obviously not asking if he could borrow my things.

"Anyway, how's college?" He asks.

"Alhamdulillah, great. How about you, am I getting a sister-in-law any sooner?" I ask, though I somewhat know the answer already.

"Shut up" He replies walking out of the door rolling his eyes.

Chapter-2: The Events.

Assalamualaikum wa rahmatullahi wa barakatuhu

Bismillah

If you haven't offered your salah and it's salah time then please pray and then return, do not delay your prayers.

MAIRA

Saturday came by early, the speech went well too. Obviously there were some weird looks from people but I didn't let them effect me, I tried at the least.

"You did great Maira! The speech was wonderful." Mrs.Henley had commented after the workshop.

This complement lead to another favour, precisely, another speech on a technical talk.

I obviously didn't expect myself to get this familiarized with Mrs.H enley in this semester, but I guess unlike other people, she saw the capabilities of the students rather than judging them by their attire, which was a good thing.

So my first semester in university was filled with all new experiences. Now, here we are coming out after writing the last exam for this semester.

The coming week was going to be packed up with full of events - cultural fest, sports on two days, sports gathering on the third day and an end of semester gathering.

To say I was not excited would be an understatement. Costumes and dresses were being decided and practices for the performances were being done.

(◍•ᴗ•◍)

Finally, the very first event that is the cultural event. All of us were supposed to be dressed according to any culture.

I picked out a white kaaftaan embedded with golden pearls on it. I also had a gold hijab with a niqab which would go perfectly with this outfit.

Zainab wore a simple blue saree, while Amina went with a flowy grey gown.

When we arrived at the place, it was all filled so we sat on the stone-benches a bit farther from the stage but we got a clear view of all the performances happening there.

There were also a few people standing across the chairs placed there. Many of our seniors dressed in different types of cultural outfits. And a very familiar figure whose back was facing me but the thick black silky hair was enough to bring back all the unwanted thoughts in my head.

I hadn't seen him this whole semester, not that I kept looking for him.

Perhaps he was in a different block.

When I glanced again at the same spot, he wasn't there anymore. Am I hallucinating? There were other people still there who were standing with him before some while so probably not hallucination.

Averting my gaze I focused back on the cultural dance that was going on there. After a few of the cultural performances, they gave us a break which was coincidentally the time for the zuhr prayer. Me and my friends go into a girls room and performed our zuhr salah. It's so good to actually have this room in our campus. Other girls come here to study during their exams, while others use it as a green room during events like these and other Muslim girls come here to offer salah occasionally.

We head to the canteen to have our lunch and just as we were going, I happened to turn back to see a bunch of people going in the same direction as ours.

And.....suprise! surprise!

There was that vintaged glass' guy talking and laughing with the others around him.

We headed straight to the counter to order our stuff. My two friends were oblivious to the presence of those people just next to us on the counter, whereas I was perfectly aware of their presence across us.

Just out of curiosity, I turned to glance at the group and just as I turned, I saw a pair of black eyes looking back at me, which were obviously not of the vintage glass' guy. I quickly turned back to my friends who were now into a conversation about the performances which happened earlier at the event.

What was I even expecting?!

A fantasy...where the female protagonist would accidently look at the male protagonist, and he would already be looking at her and they would lock their eyes for a mere second and both of them would quickly avert their gazes.....HUH how typical?!

Trust me! The amounts of fantasies going inside my head are utmost!

"Heyy!! Take your tray up" Zainab nudged my shoulder bringing me out of my trance.

Way to embarrass yourself Maira.

We went to the farthest corner of the hall where there is a wall on the right side which makes it comfortable eating in a cafetaria by moving my niqab to my left side and having the wall cover on the right side. This is also the last table in this corner because of which there is no table in front of us.

"So we are coming directly on the sports meet right?" asks Amina.

Both of us nod our heads in agreement and continued having our food.

There were only sports activities happening on these two days so we had previously decided to skip these days and sleep at home but for some reason I was actually having second thoughts about not coming to college these two days. I pushed those thoughts aside and decided that sleep was still a better option nevertheless.

On the way out of the canteen I saw that the certain group of people were still there having their food, while the vintage glass' guy was typing away something in his phone. Who even checks out their phone while eating? And why on earth am I even looking at him?

Astagfirullah!!!!

As I quickly tried to avert my gaze, a girl sitting just beside him saw me or was she already looking at me all the while?

Did she catch me staring at the guy who was beside her? Ya Allah!!

But why is she not scowling at me like she should, if someone stares at her boyfriend or something.

"You know, they both are siblings" Zainab said looking in the same direction where I had been looking.

"Oh yeah, I remember her from the freshers's day, she was the host right?"

"How did I not recognise her?" I thought out loud.

'Because you were shamelessly gawking at a certain vintaged glass guy who is also co-incidentally her own brother' my subconscious reminded me.

"You didn't? I taught you actually knew her and that's why you were looking towards her" Zainab said furrowing her eyebrows

"And that is if you were looking for someone else there?" commented Amina wiggling her eyebrows.

"Yeah right..." I brushed them off and began walking towards the event area. Luckily now there were chairs empty, we sat on the middle rows and just after some while the same event continued.

Eventually the space started to fill up and the vintage glass' boy and his group sat a bit more in the front of us. I couldn't see him completely, but I could see his hair and his hands when he would rake his fingers through them.

Shaking my head at how haraam I am sounding to gawk at a non-mehram, I tried to pay my attention to my friends.

"Do you think she is looking over here?" Zainab asked pointing to the other side of the area, I saw the girl whom Zainab told was HIS SISTER.

Ya Allah why on earth is she looking this way, or more precisely...me!!

'Did she really see me looking at her brother?'!!

Hopefully not.

Thinking this I looked back to the place where the vintaged glass guy was sitting and he wasn't there.

Ugh..Not this again.

Frowning I looked to the left side and found him looking at me......
.wait WHAT!!!

Before I could comprehend anything, he looked back to the stage, but his friend who was standing beside him looked quite familiar and...and...and... he was the same black eyed guy back in the canteen.

But what caught me off guard was the fact that the vintaged glass guy had looked back at me again and averted his gaze again.

I obviously didn't think that the fantasy of mine would happen like this.

"Guys I'm getting bored, this thing is already coming to an end anyway..." Amina said yawing.

"Yeah, my brother said that he would pick me up now, we are supposed to go somewhere after this." Zainab agreed showing her complete dis-interest in staying anymore.

"Okay, then... we'll leave." I agreed though I didn't want to leave this early.

Chapter-3: The Sport's Meet.

MAIRA

Coming back home, I saw that Mama was asleep, I showered and prayed for a bit more extra time....knowing that I had committed way to many sins today. You know the way that guilt floods back after committing a sin...yes exactly like that.

"Salam crackhead! Didn't come down yet?" That was Usman.

"Oh, so I am now a crackhead for just not coming down. Huh?"

"How was your day anyway? You had some event today right?"

"Oh, I'm actually surprised that you remember. And it was good Alhamdulillah."

He came from the couch to lay on my bed and to take my laptop from me.

"Hey, what's with you and taking my laptop and I was actually doing something on it now."

I said retrieving back my laptop from him.

"I was just curious to see what you were doing in there." He said pointing at the laptop which was successfully with me.

"What's there to be curious about this, unless... you want to see Mariam's latest pictures?" I asked wiggling my eyebrows.

Apparently my brother had a tiny bit crush on Mariam and the look on Mariam's face when I told her this gave a clear indication that my brother's feelings were completely requited. But both of them deny and say that it was a long time back and its nothing as such now.

As though I'm going to believe them, huh!

"Of course not, why would I want to see her?" he asked turning a bit red.

"Perhaps, because she didn't come here in a long time and you're desperate to have her one glance." I said grinning and giving him an 'I know it all' look.

"Oh shut up, will you? Coming to your room was a mistake I guess." He said getting up from the bed and leaving the room.

"Whatever helps you sleep at night." I yelled back at his retreating figure.

I was then called down to have dinner and then came back up and slept peacefully after an eventful yet an uneventful day.

(◉•‿•◉)

"Maira, if you do not wake up this second wallahi you're gonna be drenched in water."

Ya Allah why should my brother be having a day-off on the same day as mine.

"How about you leave my room this second?" I asked irritation crawling in.

"Not happening sister! Come on, wake up" he said truly enjoying my state.

"Okay I will, now go"

"Say wallahi"

"Seriously brother?"

"Seriously sister" He said smirking.

"Wallahi now go"

Muttering under my breath, I dragged my feet to the bathroom.

After getting freshened up for the day I went down to have my breakfast.

"Mama you didn't had to stay without eating, waiting for me." I said as we both sat down for breakfast.

"It's fine honey, these are the days when we get to have breakfast together"

"Awww" that was Usman.

"Is someone jelly jelly?" I asked smirking.

"You and I both know that mama loves me more, so why would I be 'jelly jelly'." He said mocking me in the last part.

"That's why she didn't have her breakfast with you, is it Usmaan?"

"What are you guys, seven?" mama asked in an exhausting voice.

"One of us is." said Usmaan looking towards me.

"Yeah and it is you" I said narrowing my eyes at him.

"You guys stop or I leave my breakfast unfinished and go to my room." Mama said completely giving upon us.

"Okay...okay" we both said together.

Usmaan went back to scrolling his phone and me to my food.

(⊞•ᴗ•⊞)

"So you're telling me that you were actually checking that guy out, weraring a niqab all the while." said Mariam through the screen, not even hiding the accusing tone in her voice.

"Dude you are not helping her exactly by saying that" Alina said being the supporter of the victim as always.

"Yeah and I do already feel a lot guilty for what I did and by the way let us not forget the fact that it was him who was coming into my view all the time." I said in my defense.

"Yeah right, so you check out every person who comes into your view, huh?" Mariam said again making me feel guilty all over again.

"Okay, now tell me what do I do?"

I was currently having a video chat with my life saving friends to whom I narrated the whole incident of yesterday.

"There's nothing you should specifically do, except for lowering your gaze everytime he is in your 'view' and not look for him in the first place" Mariam said more like ordered.

"I was not actually looking for him, but I do need to work on lowering my gaze." I said.

They began narrating their eventful and uneventful weeks which I heard them rant about.

It was a perfectly good idea to have a chat with them every now and then. Just looking at their stupid faces and listening to their ridiculous talks lifts up my mood.

Alhamdulillah for having these great friends.

Having a holiday means hanging around the kitchen and spending time with mama.

It's a heart warming experience to see her listen to all my rants and stuff about college. Obviously not 'that' stuff though.

(◍•ᴗ•◍)

The next day also went pretty much the same if you minus the video call and add more of mine and my brother's bickering.

Now here I am dressing up for today.

It was a sports meet and we were supposed to wear anything casual. I wore a blue casual dress with grey hijab and niqab and a pair of grey converse.

I had my breakfast and left to college.

My brother was dropping me today and I was actually thankful that he had a day off today or else I would have to take the bus.

(◍•ᴗ•◍)

I don't know how I always manage to be the last one in the three of us. It seems that they were waiting for more than ten minutes for me.

All the sport's activities had gotten over in the last two days except for the running races and relays.

Currently the girl's running race was going on and after this would be of the boys' and then the prize distribution.

"Hey look, the girl from the other day has also participated" Zainab said while pointing at a girl with a white jersey who was prepping herself for the race. She was quite far from where we were sitting.

"Which girl?" I asked trying to see her face more clearly.

"That guy's sister over here" Amina said now pointing to our left side.

And there he was, whom I was so not planning on seeing today at all. In a light blue jersey and black tracks.

Why didn't I already figure out when Zainab said the girl from yesterday? And why am I still looking at him? I was just thinking all this that he turned his head towards our side.

I quickly turned my head and wished that he just didn't see me looking at him.

Oh Allah, now I just wish for the ground to open up and swallow me whole.

I looked back at the races happening on the ground, eventually the girls' race got over and now it was the time for the boys' race.

The same sky blue jersey came into my view.

Of course he had to be in the race!

I lowered my gaze and stared at the screen of my phone.

"We are here to watch the events, not your phone" Amina said taking away the phone from my hands.

"Give it back, I will keep it in inside" I tried getting it back.

"Not happening" she exclaimed keeping it in her bag.

I sighed looking everywhere but the ground, there were two girls having bars of chocolate and a packet of chips.

"I should probably go buy something to eat." I said feeling it would be a good excuse.

"No, wait we'll go together after this. This is the last match and its relay, I thought you liked it." Zainab said.

"Yeah, I do but I guess I'll just go." I said glancing towards the ground.

Damn.

Why should he wear such a bright colour which could literally be seen from everywhere?

"Oh, sit down" Amina pulled me to sit back again.

"We'll go after this, okay?"

"Yeah, I guess." I gave in finally.

I couldn't help but wander my eyes back to the ground.

He had removed his glasses now probably to run more comfortably.

The race started.

A person holding a relay stick had to run all the way to the other person on the other end and hand him the stick. It goes on until all the four people have have ran and the fourth person of every group completes the race.

The vintaged glass' guy -who currently didn't have his glasses on- was in the second position and as soon as the first guy handed him the stick, he ran towards the third person. And just as he handed him the stick, he tripped and fell completely scratching his elbows on the ground.

"Shit" I muttered inwardly.

"Damn, that was a bad fall, wasn't it?" asked Amina from beside me.

"Yeah" Zainab agreed.

I also hummed in response, though my gaze was fixed on him, he stood up with the help of his friend and looked at the race expectantly.

And just when the forth boy of his team finished the race before everyone else, he pumped his fist in the air out of happiness but just the next second he winced bringing his hand down rubbing the wounded elbow.

"Huhh, done, now come let's go to have some good food." Amina said bringing my gaze back to her.

We then thought it would be better if we first finish with our Salahs.

So after finishing our prayers we bought some snacks and came near a very secluded corner of our college. There was grass on this area and many trees giving shade. It was perfect to just sit here, eat food and relax.

"This place is so good, I don't even feel like going back to the ground area anymore." Amina said lying her head on her bag.

"Yeah, let's just stay here. We anyway don't have anything to do there."
Zainab said already leaning on her bag and lying down.

I kept munching on my chips, thinking why I could not make myself
agree to sitting here and just chilling.

After finishing my chips, I searched my bag to find my phone.

"Give my phone back. You still have it with you right?" I asked remembering Amina hadn't returned it to me yet.

"Yeah, I do" she said and straightened up.

"We'll just go now, shall we?" Zainab asked getting up too.

"I don't think so you'll need it now that we are going" Amina stated.

I sighed.

"Fine keep it with yourself." I said.

We came back to the ground to see that the prize distribution was still
going on, but very few students were present which means that it was
coming to an end.

We sat as comfortably as we could, across the ground on the stone
benches.

Just then my phone started ringing, Amina groaned.

"I should've given it to you already" she said and dug into her bag for my phone.

The moment she handed me the phone, it stopped ringing.

"All this effort for nothing" she exaggerated.

I took the phone and opened to see an unknown number's missed call.

Just as I was about to call back, it ringed again with the same number.

"Hello" I said.

"Hi, is this Maira I'm speaking to?' asked a girl's voice.

"Yes, it is"

"Maira, Miss. Henley has asked for you to meet her in the staff room?"

"Yeah?" I asked unsure of the suddenness.

"Yeah and she asked you to hurry up, okay?" her voice sounded urgent.

"Yeah, okay I'm coming."

I discnnected the call and turned towards my friends.

"Miss. Henley has called, so I'll just be back. Okay?" I asked getting up.

"Okay. Call us, if you need anything." Zainab called out.

I showed them a thumbs up and proceeded towards the staff room. It was on the first floor.

It was clear that there were no other students because of the silence. I wonder what help she would need now.

I walked into the corridor , there were three classrooms and one staff room on this floor.

Just as I passed the first room, I was pulled into the door of second room.

I closed my eyes just for a second before opening it again to see the vintage glass' guy standing in front of me as my back was pressed to the door.

He still held my hand which he pulled previously, and was too very close for my liking.

My heart was beating erratically and I was 100% sure that he was able to hear it.

He sighed and my gaze was stuck at his face.

Oh God!

Chapter - 4: The Talk.

M AIRA

"Now tell me, what's up with you?" he asked looking at my face or eyes as a matter of fact.

His eyes are grey with those blue flecks in it and his voice...Ya Allah, I would be profusely lying if I say that his voice is not attractive. Not just attractive but even husky and for some reason I want to hear more of it.

"Shouldn't I be asking you the same question?" I questioned him back with the left out strength in me.

He didn't answer but just kept looking at me.

I tried to remove his hold on my hand, he withdrew his hand and moved a step back raking his fingers in those hair, again. I exhaled audibly when he moved a bit farther.

All this chaos was sort of suffocating me but I wanted him to answer. And I am getting insane because of all these thoughts.

I also need to leave this place, immediately.

"Were you not stealing glances at me on the other day?"

Shit!

Ya Allah please send the angel of death already before I would've to answer him.

"I... I guess you're mistaken" I stuttered.

"You and I both know that I'm not." he said coming closer.

"You are. What made you think that I would do so?" I asked getting freaked out because of the proximity.

"You want to know what?" he asked, rhetorically.

"Look at how hard it's beating." he said grabbing hold of my hand and placing it on my heart, never leaving my hand again.

I lowered my gaze from his eyes and settled them on my hand held by his.

"Oh, don't feel embarrassed, here..."he shifted my hand upon his heart, which was erratically beating. Perhaps, even harder than mine.

"This is the effect of your presence near me..." he said causing me to lower my eyes.

"Not just now suddenly but from quite a while." he added gaining my gaze yet again.

'What on earth does he mean by "from quite a while"?' I thought to myself.

"Yes Maira, its not just now that I've noticed you" he answered as though hearing my thoughts.

And did he just say my name? Damn...it felt more than good to hear it and damn it if I didn't want to hear it again.

He removed my hand from his heart but didn't leave it, he rubbed circles on the back of my palm with his thumb.

My heart pounded even more aggressively.

I wriggled my hand from his, which caused him to tighten his grip.

"Just listen to me." He said

I shook my head

"I'm not obliged to and you're not supposed to touch me, hell...We're not supposed to be in here in the first place." I said raising a bit of my voice.

"Okay, I won't touch you." He raised his hands up.

"But listen to me first" he placed his hands on the door on the either sides of my head.

He is tall...!!!

"Please" he added softly.

"I've admired you from the day I've heard about you, I guess it was the very first week of college. People talked about the girl who covers her face and whose face nobody has seen. I was curious about you even though I hadn't seen you. Then one day when me and my friends were watching the video of the technical talk...there you were confidently giving the speech. You didn't seem to care about what the people would say if they look at you. You surely weren't insecure about your attire or anything. I had even seen you at the fresher's party and to say that I was surprised to see you with the niqab even then would be an understatement. I so... wanted to know you more, talk to you and what not. The other day I saw you when you were in the canteen when your friends were having a conversation with you. Just after you left my sister told me that there was a girl who she thought was stealing glances at me, I was not interested until she mention that the girl wore a white dress with a niqab. She then showed me who it was ...it was you. I instantly denied telling her that she was delusional you know what did she say?" he asked smiling and then slightly chuckling, his eyes sparkled and cheeks turned slightly pink.

"She said that even I wanted you to notice me somehow. She was right though, I couldn't deny the fact that some part of my heart did want you to notice me and speak to you." He whispered the last part coming incredibly close to my ear.

I was utterly shocked to hear his whole narrative. But more than that I was very much aware of our situation here and none of all this was right.

"Say something, please" he said looking into my eyes.

"All this is not right, looking at you, even for a moment was a sin and I don't want you or myself to get involved in any kind of these sins." I said shaking my head and trying to move.

"Listen, I am not going against anything you say, if anything you've got me back on my Deen. I just want to know you. The curiousness which I have about you is just.. a lot." He said.

"You're crazy, what do you mean by you want to know me, I am not a research project or anything." I said getting annoyed.

I guess Allah is just punishing me for the sins I've done in these past days.

Now, I regret every moment when I looked up at him, instead of lowering my gaze.

"I am very much motivated by the way you carry your Deen in this society, the progress which I've made just by looking at you is insane. I think that when you don't give a damn about the society and live just to please Allah, then how hard could it be for me." He said causing stupid flips in my heart.

"Then you should be the one who should understand my morals more than anyone. How could you think that I would be okay talking to a stranger in this closed room? I know that I'm at fault too for starting this in the first place and trust me, I regret it. After everything said and done, all this is still wrong. Hell...I don't even know your name as a matter of fact." I said realizing the same.

"Adam, that's my name" he said lowly causing those butterflies in my belly which people always talk about.

"That was not the point of the whole thing which I said"

He couldn't act like he didn't even hear the first part of my sentence.

(⫲•‿•⫲)

ADAM

How am I even gonna say her that I am drawn to her, for the way she lowers her eyes every time she feels embarrassed or the way she is so firm in her Deen.

The fact that I am ready to sit here just gazing in her eyes for my entire life nearly scares me. I wonder the impact she would have upon me in the future, when just now I'm willing to experience the sweetness of my Deen just by looking at her firmness in it.

"You make me want to be a good person, you make me want to feel closer to Allah." I said finally, she didn't say anything, so I continued.

"I feel like I can---." I was cut off by her ringing phone.

She glanced at it and then at me.

Her eyes seemed confused, though I don't know what the confusion it was about.

She silenced the call and tried to unlock the door but I kept my hand on it refusing to let her go.

She looked back at me, her eyes...I felt that I would give up my entire life for those orbs of her's.

I let her go.

I knew I had to.

My respect for her and her Deen encompassed the admiration which I had for her.

And above everything else, it was what was right to do, as she likes to call it.

Perhaps, she was just a means Allah had sent to get me on the straight path.

And being on the straight path doesn't mean me to go after her, it means for me to go after my Deen and closer to Allah.

Chapter-5: Holidays.

MAIRA

"I'm going to bed Mama, Ma'salaam" I said going up to my room and plopping down on the bed.

It's been more than two weeks after that particular incident. And I'm grateful that we have holidays.

Who knows if he would again confront me or something? Though I doubt that he would do so.

'You make me want to be a good person, you make me want to feel closer to Allah'

His words have been creating chaos in my head from the past two weeks.

His words have caused flips in my heart which I never have experienced before. A pinch of admiration had been built inside my heart for him, when he let me go and respected my space.

The incident on that day was a true outcome of my doings. And I've promised myself to not get involved in these sins again inshaAllah.

All these thoughts have been going in my head and I'm not able to get myself to narrate my thoughts to anyone.

Not even to Mariam and Alina, though they have figured out that there' something off with me. And they've decided a meet over would do. So they're coming tomorrow to stay here for a day or two.

(◍•ᴗ•◍)

"Its good that Alina's parents let her go easily, otherwise she wouldn't be here with her forgetting skills." Mariam said causing me to laugh and Alina to scowl.

Apparently all three of us are in my car and we're going to my place after me picking them up from the station earlier. And Mariam was describing Alina's famous 'forgetting skills' of how Alina completely forgot to tell her parents that she is coming over to my place for a couple of days.

"Here we are" I said out loud parking the car in front of the house.

"Is Usmaan home? I'm sure our sweet Mariam here would be desperate to see him again after so long." Alina teased Mariam in a quite loud voice.

"Unfortunately, he isn't. But don't worry he'll be back soon." I said helping them take their stuff from the trunk.

"Why do you guys have to even bring him in our conversations?" Mariam asked slightly frustrated.

"Salam sweeties!" mama exclaimed opening the door.

"Salam Aunty" both of them said entering the house.

"Its so good to see you guys again"

"Yeah, it's good to see you too Aunty" Alina agreed with mama.

"I'm sure you must be bored to continuously live with this idiot here" Mariam said flipping my forehead.

"Hey, I'm her daughter, don't you forget that." I said quite dramatically.

"Yeah, can't help." Mama teased shaking her head which caused both of my friends to laugh.

(⦿•‿•⦿)

"Okay now, spill up." Mariam said sitting on my bed taking a bite of the cookie that Mama had given us on our way up to the room.

Now what do I say to these guys?

"And lying is haraam." Alina said reminding me.

I guess I'll just tell them later.

"And don't even think of saying 'some time later' or 'not now', just tell us what it is that's really bothering you." Alina said in a worrisome voice.

These people know me just too well.

"You remember that vintaged glass' guy I told you about?" I asked anxiously.

"Don't tell me you messed yourself up in that" Mariam said pointedly.

"No, it was him who initiated it on that day."

"Do we have to buy some wooden bats and hockey sticks to teach him some lessons?" Alina asked exaggeratedly fisting up her hands.

"What? No! It's not how it sounds like." I said trying to explain my point.

"Then tell us" Mariam said in a hurried tone.I narrated to them the whole ordeal of that day.

And their comments were like this,

Adam! That's a nice name.Are you really sure that those butterflies weren't because you were hungry or something right?In which hand did he wear his watch?He's really good with his words!Wow!! Blue flecks in grey eyes... But you were supposed to lower your gaze right?

"That's it? He didn't try to get to you after that at all?" Alina asked arching a brow.

"I had holidays after that day. I... I mean not exactly after that day..I didn't go on the end of semester gathering though." I said looking down.

"Scaredy cat"

"You didn't go on an event because you were scared that you would see him again."

Both of them said shaking their heads.

"I just didn't know what else to do" I said finally letting out my thoughts.

Mariam sighed.

I sighed.

Alina sighed.

"Look, it's okay, you'll be fine once your mind gets distracted from that stuff." Mariam said assuringly.

"Yeah you've been locked up in your house ever since. I can't believe that you spent two weeks of your holidays doing exactly nothing in your home" Alina said.

"So we'll go out have some food and enjoy!" Mariam yelled putting on her abaya and niqab.

Chapter - 6: Leaving.

MAIRA

"Girls are you coming down for dinner or you'll just have it up here?" mama asked poking her head through the door.

"Is Usmaan home mama?" I asked glancing towards Mariam, slyly.

"Yes but he will be okay to have his dinner in his room if you guys are coming down" mama answered.

"No, its fine aunty we'll be okay in the room itself" Mariam spoke before anyone of us could.

"Are you sure?" mama asked, unconvincingly.

"Yes aunty, shukran!" Mariam replied smiling.

"Shy to go face the love of your life?" Alina teased Mariam as soon as mama left.

"Give up already, all this is getting really old for a joke" Mariam replied in an exhausted tone.

"The color of your cheeks says otherwise" I commented poking her cheeks.

"You know what? I am leaving" Mariam said swatting my hand away and getting up.

"So that you could see Usmaan there, huh?" Alina asked wiggling her eyebrows.

"Guys stop, I'll go get dinner from downstairs" I said going towards the door and opening it.

"Coming?" I asked Mariam grinning.

"Get lost!" she threw the pillow just as I closed the door.

(◍•ᴗ•◍)

"I do not want you guys to go tomorrow" I said lying down on the bed between them

"Aww, is someone mushy?" Mariam asked.

"I do not want to either dude, it's the same old life again." Alina said sighing.

"I'm worried about going back to college after this week" I said looking at ceiling.

"I don't think so he'll want to talk to you." Alina said turning towards me.

"And why is that?" Mariam asked from beside me.

"He wouldn't have let her go on that day if he would want to see her again" Alina said sitting up.

"Honestly, I also think the same thing" I said sitting up too.

"He respected your privacy and space, he understood your morals, he wouldn't disrupt it, out of all people" Alina said nodding her head.

"Yeah, but what if he accidentally appears in front of me?"

"He wont , and even if he appears, act normal. Go to college, study or do whatever you always do and come back home. Its just a matter of some days until you get back to normalcy." Mariam reasoned.

I laid back down nodding.

These two days were indeed a distraction from all the chaotic thoughts running in my head.

We had been to shopping, having food at different places and having makeover session and hair styling at midnight while eating all sorts of food. But like every good thing comes to an end, all this is also ending. Both of them are leaving tomorrow morning and I have my college opening in a week.

(◍•ᴗ•◍)

"Maira, baba is calling you in the leaving room" Usmaan says peeking through the door.

"Why is baba here wo early? It's not even 7" baba comes back only after 9, unless its some emergency.

"He just is, so hurry. I'm curious about what he has to say" Usmaan says hurriedly.

I wrap a hijab loosely around my head and walk with my brother to the living room.

"Salam baba" I say as I see him.

"Salam sweetie, come sit with us." baba says pointing towards the empty couch across him.

Usman takes a sit just on the opposite couch from mine while mama is already seated next to baba.

Baba clears his throat.

"So yesterday after the Ishaa salah a man approached me at the mosque asking me if I was Abdul Haseeb, the father of Maira Abdul Haseeb" baba said looking up at me.

I confusedly looked towards Usmaan who himself was giving me a look which tells 'what on earth is going on?'.

I just shrugged my shoulders and looked back at baba.

"He has put forward a... umm... a marriage proposal of his son with you. He said that his daughter studies in the same university as yours and she is a friend of yours who is actually the one who initially came up with this when he was having a discussion with his family." Baba says again looking back at me. I instantly looked down towards my feet.

Seriously, what on earth is going on?

Proposal for marriage! Oh Allah.

Who is even this girl because as far as I know most of my friends have brothers in their primary school and others don't even have any brothers.

"He said that he and his family would come over to see you if you and all of us are fine with it" baba says sharing a look with mama and then looks at me expectantly.

what am I supposed to even say?

"Me and your mama have discussed this matter but before we tell you anything, we want to hear your opinion."

"I... I" I stuttered and looked down at my hands on lap.

"Baba lets give her sometime, I'm sure she'll be able to give her opinion by the morning." Usmaan spoke.

Alhamdulillah that I've got him.

"Okay then, tomorrow morning at breakfast?" baba asked

I just nodded my head and straightly went to my room.

"That was one of a talk, huh?" Usmaan asked getting inside my room.

"What am I supposed to do or say? I am completely clueless about all of this." I said stressing on the whole sentence.

"It's fine if you feel this, although it would've been an issue if you felt just normal" he said reassuringly.

"So what do you suggest that I should say to baba?"

"I guess you should give it a shot, it won't be your final decision, you can surely deny the proposal straight away but first let them come see you and take help from Allah to help in your every decision"

This is the most serious conversation I've ever had with Usmaan.

I guess I will give this proposal a shot.

"Can you tell to baba that I'm okay with the people coming over to see me?" I asked nervously.

"Sure princess" Usmaan teased pulling me in a side hug.

Chapter-7: The Proposal.

MAIRA

I never thought that the people who were coming over were that desperate, because they decided to meet just a day after the evening baba told them that we're okay with taking this alliance or whatever it is a bit further.

It's not that I don't like them coming to see me or anything, I guess it's just too sudden.

Now here I am getting myself prepared mentally and physically. Mama told that even if I don't come in front of everyone there, the mother and the sister of that particular person would surely want to see me. And I don't think that they are obviously going to just see me in my niqab.

Nervous? Of course I am.

I just wish that either Mariam or Alina should've been here. Apparently they've classes and many other previously planned stuff. Both of them were more excited than me after hearing about the whole 'coming over to see me' fiasco. They went to the extent of deciding the name of the kids I would have. Acting as if they know it all. What if the people coming to see me doesn't approve of me wearing a niqab? I've heard enough judge-mental gossips about me wearing a niqab to get this possibility in my head. What if the guy doesn't really like a religious girl?

It would be ridiculous that I don't even know the name of the guy whom I'm probably seeing to get married if everything works out well by the will of Allah. It's not that I didn't try getting to know his name, but Usmaan won't tell me even though he knows it. And I'm too timid to ask mama or baba.

I hear different voices from downstairs and my palms become sweatier.

"Sweetie they're all here and Adam's mother and sister will be in the dining area soon." Mama says standing near the door of my room.

ADAM?

That does sound like a very familiar name.

I couldn't just randomly forget that name anytime soon.

Could it be THE ADAM?

There are certainly many reasons for this Adam to be him but it could also just be my stupid conscience.

I don't know if I'm actually okay with the probability of this Adam being that particular Adam.

I think--

"Maira come down before they come in the dining area" mama said interrupting my thoughts.

I nod my head in affirmative and follow her to the dining room.

Mama asks me to pour juice in the glasses and leaves to call them here.

Could this be really that Adam?

Before I could answer my own question I hear footsteps coming towards the dining room where I am present right now.

My hands become sweatier as I struggle to pour the juice.

I pray silently to Allah to help me get through this whole thing, no matter who the person is.

"Assalamualaikum wa rahmatullahi wa barakatuhu!" I heard an elderly voice while my back was still turned towards them.

"Walaikumassalam wa rahmatullahi wa barakatuhu aunty" I said smiling turning towards them.

She was in a black abaya and a maroon hijab with a genuine smile on her face.

Just then mama and another girl entered the dining area.

It is definitely that Adam!

Allah whatever sort of thing this is with which you are testing, please help me!

"Assalamualaikum" she exclaimed smiling widely as if she was seeing me for the first time, well technically she is.

"Walaikumassalam" I replied glancing towards her and then quickly looking towards mama.

My heart rate was drastically increasing while my mind was slowly registering the current scenario.

"Come let's sit here" mama said walking towards the chairs.

I sat on the chair just beside mama while both of them sat across us.

"I understand that all this is quite sudden to all of you but when we started the talk of Adam's marriage he seemed a bit hesitant and then Aisha came up with your suggestion and we saw how Adam silently agreed to it, although he didn't say anything and that is the reason we put forward this proposal." The aunty spoke -whose name I didn't know yet-.

So his sister's name was Aisha.

And I definitely heard everything other than her name. So they don't know about the little encounter I had with her son the other day. But I'm certain that his sister knows because her little smile is really suggestive and now when I think about it I'm quite sure that it was her who called me saying that Miss. Henley had asked for me.

I lift my head up to see all the three women staring back at me. Ya Allah, how did I even zone out in this situation?

"Maira, why don't you take Aisha upstairs to your room and have a little friend's talk?" mama asked eyeing me pointedly clearly leaving no room for disagreement.

"Sure, come on" I said looking towards Aisha and getting up.

I opened the door to my room thinking about the awkwardness we both are going to face.

What are even supposed to speak about?

Aisha enters behind me and closes the door.

Okayy.

"Look I know this is going to be a hell lot of awkward and you would have thousands of questions to ask. But before you ask anything, I'll myself clear it out for you." She said in a single breath.

I nodded my head slowly saying a quiet okay.

"Let's sit here first" I said motioning towards the end-of-bed cushion bench.

"The first thing which my brother said to tell you was sorry." she says as soon as she sits.

I furrow my eyebrows. Sorry?

"Yes, he is sorry for behaving the way he behaved on the other day in the classroom though he wouldn't tell me exactly what he did." She said feigning annoyance causing me to smile lightly.

"He is also sorry for bringing this proposal to you, not that he didn't want to, it's just that he doesn't want to enforce you into something you don't want to do." She reasoned.

I just hummed, not knowing what to say exactly.

"He never wanted to impede in your privacy but when baba started the topic of his marriage he couldn't get himself to say anything." She continued.

"I asked him later as to why he behaved the way he did, he said that he was not ready for any sort of commitment like that but just after a second of saying that he shook his head as though realizing something and then saying it was not the actual reason. He said that he could not get off his mind from you to think about someone else."

She said grinning and nudging my shoulder and I felt my face heat up.

She doesn't have to say every detail.

"But he didn't want to drag you in all of this but I talked him out and told him that we'll first try to give this alliance a chance before ending it even before beginning it." she finished sighing exaggeratedly.

"Come on, say something" she spoke again.

A feeling of déjà vu surged through me of her brother.

I shook my head slightly, in an attempt to remove his picture from my thoughts.

"All this is so sudden that I don't even know what to think anymore" I said.

"I know, I can understand how difficult it would be for you but one thing that I can say is that my brother is totally whipped for you" she said causing me to lower my eyes.

"Take your time and give your answer, you might as well do istikhara to seek Allah's help. I don't want to persuade you into saying yes at all, it's your decision to make and Adam will accept it truly with his heart."

Chapter-8: The Wait.

A DAM

I tap my feet nervously on the carpet of Maira's living room where we are seated right now.

The calculative and quite intimidating gaze of Usmaan who is apparently Maira's brother isn't helping at all. I wonder if I looked the same way as him when Yusuf brought a proposal for Aisha. Aisha says that Yusuf still feels intimidated by me although they are married.

It's been a while after Aisha and mama have left to see Maira, and I'm starting to get worried as the time is getting passed. Maira's dad and baba are having a conversation and every now then they direct a question towards me.

Hopefully Maira doesn't think badly of me to bring this proposal, I didn't want to in the first place. But I couldn't bring myself to lie to Aisha when she asked me about it. The things which I said to Maira about becoming a better person were indeed true. And I can see the changes happening within me since then.

"Dinner's ready" I hear an elderly voice, probably Maira's mom.

"Come on, lets continue the chat in the dining area" Mr. Abdul Haseeb says getting up.

All of us gather in the dining area while I hear some footsteps descending down the stairs and halting. I keep my eyes lowered to my plate all the while, and then there are hurried footsteps going up the stairs again.

(◍•ᴗ•◍)

"Won't you ask anything about the conversation I had with Maira?" Aisha asks plopping next to me on the bed.

We had returned back after an amazing dinner at their place. Mr. Abdul Haseeb said that they'll get back with an answer in a day or two. That brought out a different level of nervousness in me. I don't even know if I will be able to survive with this amount of nervousness floating in my body.

Aisha snaps her fingers in front me to get me out of my trance.

"I choose not to ask you anything." I say.

She scoffs.

"Admit that you desperately want to know what we talked, because we talked a lot of stuff." She says grinning slyly.

"Okay tell me what happened" I say slightly perking my interest.

"I don't think I want to, now" she says sticking her tongue out.

"Traitor" I feign an accusing tone narrowing my eyes.

She laughs loudly.

"She seemed to be impressed when I spoke about you." She says in a more gentle and serious voice.

Her words caused a sense of happiness in my heart.

I just shake my head to stop my mind from heightening the already heightened hopes.

I would accept her decision wholeheartedly no matter in whose favor it is.

But the wait is agonizing.

(◍•ᴗ•◍)

I walk into the university fully smiling and delightful.

Yes!!

She said yes!!

And our parents decided to not delay in taking this alliance forward but Maira wanted to talk to me before anything else. So a part of my mind is still not at peace.

I'm anxious about what she has to say but I also wonder what made her say yes to this proposal.

"You seemed to be in a good mood today bro." Jake says walking with me.

I just shrugged not wanting to say anything just now. I don't know if Maira wants to reveal this whole alliance thing yet.

Besides Jake said that Maira looked a bit suspicious by the way she dresses on that cultural event. I had instantly defended him telling that we have no right to be commenting on others attires.

I'm sure I would have said the same thing even if it was not the girl whom I'd admired but I guess it would've been a bit less defensive.

The day goes by as normally as a first day goes and now me, Jake and three other of my friends are heading to the last class of the day when Aisha comes running to go with us. Apparently she and I have a same subject on Mondays and Thursdays but she's a year younger to me. She had her nikah done last year when Yusuf's family had approached us although she will officially move in with him after she completes her University.

"Maira talked to me earlier today, she wants to speak to you over the phone by the end of the day and she has already told her parents about it." Aisha says bringing back the anxiousness which I had pushed behind.

"So she won't meet in person?" I ask her, slight disappointment in my voice.

"Aww!! The desperateness though..." she drawls before walking into the class and me trailing behind her with the chaos inside my head.

Chapter-9: InshaAllah

MAIRA

"You can always take his number and call him yourself right?" Aisha asks from beside me.

We are currently walking to sit in the secluded corner of our college where there are no other people to disturb my conversation with Adam.

Aisha's words not mine!

This day definitely didn't go as any normal day. I narrated the whole proposal thing to Amina and Zainab, just the proposal thing not the incidents on the sport's day or anything before the proposal. They were utterly surprised by the sudden revelation, however, they didn't seem much suspicious about the fact that the guy is from our university. They just were too shocked to comprehend anything else. I don't blame them though I would've had an equally same reaction if one of my friends suddenly emerges with a proposal.

"What will be the whole point of chaperoning when you give me his number to talk?" I ask her back.

"You guys don't need chaperoning in the first place!" she exclaims looking towards me.

I just shake my head and go ahead to sit on the grass.

"I wonder why no one comes to this place because it's amazing and so good to take a break from the whole studying thing." Aisha sits on the grass making herself comfortable.

I just smile and sit down leaning my back a little.

"So...shall we?" she asks sitting down too and taking out her phone.

All the anxiousness came back rushing which I had pushed back earlier. It's not that I don't want to speak to him. I have a couple of questions which sound silly and ridiculous but I don't think so I could go ahead in this alliance without knowing their answers.

I just nod at Aisha to call her brother. I would've passed out of anxiousness if I had to talk to him in person. I guess both of us would be be more comfortable if we talk on phone.

"Asslamualaikum brother" Aisha says causing my heart rate to increase and palms to sweat.

She eyes me asking if I'm ready to talk. I just nod knowing that this has to be done.

I grab the phone with my cold hands and put the call on speaker.

"Just so you don't blab out anything, your dear Maira here have put the call on speaker" she says to Adam rolling her eyes with a sly grin.

"I wouldn't Aisha" a very familiar and incredibly beautiful voice says, stirring up some unknown emotions in me.

He then clears his throat.

"Assalamualaikum...Maira" he says bringing back my longing desire to hear my name from that voice again.

"Walaikumassalam" I say in a surprisingly quiet voice.
"I believe that you had something to talk to me about?" he asks once he realizes that I wouldn't start by myself.

"I do" I say clearing my throat.

I just sigh not able to form any coherent sentence dues to my rapid heartbeat.

"We can drag this to another time if you aren't comfortable now." He says in a tender tone.

"No. I am fine... I guess" I mumble the last part more to myself causing him to chuckle.

That sound was fascinatingly alluring. I was almost going to ask him to do it again.

Almost.

"Are you sure about this...umm...thing?" I ask clearly not wanting to say any embarrassing term.

"Thing?" he asks voice laced with confusion.

"Marriage idiot. She's asking about marriage." Aisha speaks shaking her head.

"I sort of thought that!" he exclaims defensively.

"Of course you did!"

"Hey Aisha!! What are you doing there?" one of her friends calls her from a bit farther from us.

"I'll just be back ok" she says getting up and dusting her dress.

"What made you ask this question?" Adam asks after a slight pause.

"If you don't mind me asking it?" he adds hurriedly.

"Of course I don't."

"And I asked it because I think that it's hard for especially a boy to get this feeling of commitment at this young age."

He chuckles just after I finish speaking.

"I am sure about this more than anything in my life Maira. The fact that I immediately pictured you when baba asked about marriage is evidence enough about my certainty. The idea of spending an entire life with a person never popped in my head until I saw you. I know that I might not exactly be your ideal person, but I wish to become that person for you."

I just gulp awkwardly not able to say anything. He continues with a sigh.

"You're the means Allah chose to bring me back my on my deen. And it's because of Allah and you that I've become a better person. I've firmly held onto my faith on Allah and I refuse to let go of that means which Allah have sent for me." He says making me skip a heartbeat.

"I'm flattered" I say with a lighthearted chuckle.

He joins in too. This time laughing wholly.

"You are the person who, though unintentionally but truly motivated me on the path of my deen. If it wouldn't have been you then I don't know how I would have changed."

"Will you give up on your deen even if I'm not there?" I ask instinctively.

"I would never! In this short time of getting to know about my religion, I know that this is not a thing a person would leave after getting it back. And I might as well keep this as a very beautiful memory of your's" he says and I can almost hear a smile in his words.

I smile too knowing that I'm as prepared as him to start this new chapter of my life.

InshaAllah.

Chapter–10: Internals

M AIRA

"So you guys literally haven't seen each other since that day?" Mariam asks through the screen.

I just shrug.

"Did you at least get the slightest desire to see him?" Alina asks raising her eyebrows.

"Of course I got, I just didn't act upon it."

"So you are like dying to see him!!" she exclaims teasingly

"You completely rephrased my sentence" I say rolling my eyes.

"We know your inner thoughts even if you don't tell them out loud."
Mariam teases

"When are you guys coming anyway?" I ask, changing the subject.

"Next month, most probably a couple of days prior to your nikah"
Alina answers.

Yes! The nikah.

It's been a couple of days after that conversation I had with Adam. And both of our parents have decided to not delay a good thing and do the nikah in the coming month when we are having a holiday for a week. I would anyway move in with him after the official walima reception which would probably be after my graduation, so until then I would stay with mama and baba.

Baba said that it would be better if we have our nikah at the earliest, it would avoid any kind of haram stuff and we could easily attend college without any hesitation.

"Already started dreaming about your prince charming sweetheart?"
Alina asks, grinning widely.

I cover my cheeks in an attempt of hiding the obvious blush that is being formed on them.

"Maira, coming down for dinner?" Usmaan asks through the slightly opened door.

"Yup! I'll be there in five, just having a chat with Mariam" I smirk.

"And Alina" I add after he narrows his eyes.

He goes back shutting my door quite loudly muttering something along the lines of 'delusional even now'.

"Why did you have to do that?" Mariam growls causing Alina to snicker audibly.

"Ma'salam, talk to you later guys" I say giggling and then hanging up.

(◍•ᴗ•◍)

"So are you really sure about this Adam guy?" Usmaan asks putting his seat belt on.

I raise my eyebrows at his unexpected question.

"What! I'm just making sure you're okay with everything which is happening" he elaborates himself.

"So...is this some bro-sis chat which we're currently having while you're dropping me off to university?" I smile pleased with his 'protective brother' attitude.

"You know what, just forget that I asked anything at all" he says agitated.

I laugh causing him to deepen his scowl.

"Okay sorry, it's just that this side of yours is quite funny actually."

He takes a sharp turn showing his obvious annoyance.

I gasp exaggeratedly "I could've died, brother!"

He scoffs "Drama queen"

I shove his shoulder lightly.

"I am really sure about all things happening around me" I answer in a more serious voice, recalling his previous question.

"And... I guess I have something to tell you..." I trail.

I haven't told anyone except for my friends about my encounters with Adam which I had before this whole proposal thing.

"What is it?" he asks and I gulp nervously

"And please don't start anything about your stupid delusions about Mariam" he adds before I could speak.

I gasp totally amazed by his words.

My slightly aghast face changes into a smirk "That means you want to hear about her, don't you?"

"Shut up and tell me what it was that you were about to tell."

I sigh.

"Okay... so maybe you might slightly freak out after hearing this?" my words comes out questioningly.

He glances towards me for a split second before turning back to the road "Just spill already!!"

I narrate the whole occurrence gauging his reaction. He looks completely startled by my words, raising his eyebrows a few times, but he lets me continue nevertheless.

"Well he is very good in acting then, because he didn't seem to know any of this when he came with his family the other day." Usmaan says in a playful tone.

I relax visibly.

"It's good that he carried it out in a mature way rather than pulling out some dumb stunts." He explains with a tint of appreciation.

I just hum in response "Here we are" he exclaims stopping near the gate of the university.

"Ma'salam" I take my bag from the seat.

"Don't assume that we are done with this conversation" He fake glares after bidding a goodbye.

(◍•ᴗ•◍)

"Why do we have our internals just after our semester has started?" Amina exclaims getting out of the classroom.

"It's good that we at least have holidays after the internals." Zainab says following us down the hallway.

"Yeah, that is the thing that will keep me motivated to do better" I agree.

"Not to forget the exclusive nikah" Amina teases.

Zainab nudges my shoulder teasingly "Right!!!"

Alhamdulillah that I have my niqab on, because my face definitely a shade of red.

"So...when are we meeting up to study?" I ask discreetly changing the subject.

"Do not try to change the topic, alright?" Amina says pointedly.

Well, not that discreetly I guess.

"But that was an important question, when are we doing the group study?" Zainab pipes in.

I sigh, thanking Allah "Tomorrow after college at my place?"

"I am in" Amina agrees.

"Okay I'll tell my brother not to pick me up then" Zainab says

"Which reminds me that he's waiting for me outside, bye guys!" she yells running out

Amina laughs shaking her head "Bye then" she waves walking off on her way.

I wave back walking on the opposite side.

We were informed today that we are going to have our first assessments in four days and we'll be having a week off after that.

I just want these tests to finish quickly, not because of that reason, just because we are having holidays and I will be meeting Mariam and Alina.

Yes. That's the only reason.

(◍•ᴗ•◍)

"Language Programming had always been a strenuous subject..." I stress out as we walk out of the class.

"It's at least over" Zainab exclaims fixing her hijab.

"Alhamdulillah"

Amina joins us walking down the hallway "And we have English tomorrow, so very less to worry about. Hence, we can go watch the football game going on in the ground" she starts walking towards the seats near the field area.

"Why don't we just go and sleep off in our homes?" I ask, tiredness seeping into my body.

Amina pulls me with her "Oh come on, you surely are not going to regret coming here" she exclaims eagerly.

Zainab walks beside us keeping her eyes on the game while I look around to find some empty seats for us. "Wait, is that--" she is cut short by a voice calling my name from the other side.

"Heyy Maira" Aisha calls pointing her hand to some empty spots near her.

Amina grins mischievously "Told you that you won't regret!"

I just roll my eyes trying to not look at the field at all.

It literally seems like a forever ago when I think about the situation similar to this.

"Salaam" Aisha says glancing towards us uncertainly probably wondering if she can say whatever she wants to say.

"Walaikuassalam" I reply smiling reassuringly although I'm not sure she noticed my smile.

"Walaikumasslam" Both of them say simultaneously.

"You do not need to feel unsure, Maira here have told us about your brother" Amina adds making Aisha smile wider.

"I am glad actually, I could not contain the excitement after seeing you" she says the last part looking towards me.

"Come on, let's cheer our college's team from here" she sits on an empty seat and we join her.

"You can particularly cheer for Adam though" she says winking at me.

I shove her shoulder lightly, still avoiding the field.

We then suddenly hear a timer going off causing me to look at the ground.

I am met with startled eyes elegantly guarded with a pair of vintage glasses.

Oh Allah!!

Quickly lowering my gaze, I instantly regret looking at the ground at all.

"Hey Adam! Need some water?" Aisha asks from beside me.

I guess I should just make an excuse and leave this place but that would be too obvious.

"I will just be right back" Zainab says talking to someone on her phone.

Adam comes and stands a bit farther from us on the left side talking to his friend while Amina grins nudging my shoulder on my right side.

If I wouldn't have been internally freaking out like this, I would have shoved this girl to the very end of this campus.

"Here," Aisha says handing Adam the bottle of water.

I keep my eyes trained on my lap at my slightly trembling fingers refusing to look up at him.

He clears his throat "Shukran"

"Assalamualaikum" he says after a couple of seconds probably after gulping down the water.

I look up at him to find him seated on a chair further from us, a bottle in his hand.

"Assalam--"

"Walaikumassalam" I cut him off before he could repeat himself.

"Came here to see me play?" he asks teasingly and I could almost hear a boyish smile in his voice.

My eyes go instantly wide at his question and this playful side of him.

He laughs quietly at my reaction and I look up at his face.

"I'm glad to see you here, honestly." He says smiling.

"Just her, not any of us?" Aisha asks wiggling her eyebrows.

"Shut up!!" both me and Adam say at once.

We look at each other amused by our unintended actions and he scratches his neck sheepishly.

"Aww look at the two of you, all lovey dovey" Aisha says and Amina hums mockingly.

These girls are literally giving me the worst feeling of awkwardness.

"Okay players get back here!!" the coach calls out from the field.

Adam gets up from his place and glances towards us.

"Best of luck" I say suddenly to which he just smiles and jogs over to the field.

"He is definitely going to win today" Amina says and Aisha laughs with her giving her a high five.

The timer goes off again indicating the start of the game.

Adam looks over our side again giving an enchanting smile and starting the game.

I smile even more widely just now realizing the fact that I've been smiling the whole time.

Chapter-11: The Exclusive Nikah!

M aira

"Assalamualaikum!! I am home" I exclaim closing the door behind me, our tests are finally over and Amina, Zainab and me had a little after-test celebration at Amina's house as her parents are at her grand mom's place.

I furrow my brows when I don't hear any reply, going further in the house I see no one in the kitchen too. "Mama" I call out climbing up the first step.

"Boo" Usmaan yells from behind me causing me to slip on the stair and land my butt on it.

Where on earth did he come from?

I place my hand on my chest to stop the rapid beating of my heart all the while glaring at a guffawing Usmaan.

"You have to look at your face" he says still breathless from the stupid laugh.

"Wait I will just take a picture to see the look on your face whenever I feel the need to" he says digging his hands in his pocket looking for his phone.

"Wait till I get back to you" I say narrowing my eyes at him.

"When? After you get married to Adam and give me a peaceful life" he says grinning and sitting next to me.

"You seem to have forgotten that I will only leave after the walima which is after I graduate" I say rolling my eyes.

"Oh I had completely forgotten about it" he says feigning disappointment but I could see a hint of relief in his hazel eyes. "Anyway, I am going to change. Where are mama and baba by the way?"

"Baba was back early today, so they've gone for some grocery shopping."

I hum a reply and go to quickly change into a pair of comfy PJ's because it's already nearing dinner time and whats better than having dinner in pajamas.

As I'm about to open the door, my phone buzzes from where it's lying on the bed.

MARIAM- 'Assalamualaikum, how were your tests??'

It buzzes again before I could reply.

ALINA- 'Walaikumassalam'

ALINA- 'Test? I don't remember me having any tests'

ME- 'Walaikumassalam, and Alhamdulillah all my tests went good'

ALINA- 'Oh right that question wasn't for me'

MARIAM- 'Yes genius'

I walk down the stairs replying to their texts when a sweet aroma fills my nostrils.. "Pancakes, hmm?" I ask as Usmaan flips a pancake.

"Who said it was for you?"

I raise a brow "You are going let your little sister starve while you stuff your mouth with these goodies" I say pointing towards the pile of pancakes on the counter.

"I might have to warn Adam of your little manipulative tactics before hand" he says shaking his head lightly.

He places the plate of pancakes on the kitchen island as I take the chocolate syrup from the refrigerator and sit on the chair near the island.

"So...how were your tests?" he asks taking a bite of his food.

I nod unable to speak because of the food in my mouth "Alhamdulillah, it's the first test of this semester so there was not much to worry about."

"When are your friends coming then?" he asks and I raise my eyebrows suggestively.

"I was just trying to make a civil conversation, dumbhead" he says shoving me with his shoulder.

I almost trip off the chair before I balance myself. "A civil coversation can also happen without including Maria-- my friends" I say cheekily

He rolls his eyes and goes for the last pancake on the plate.

No way!

I put my fork on the pancake too.

"I cooked them so I deserve to have them" Usmaan says attempting to take it.

"You have already had enough to last for a month, so I am having this"

"I am a growing person and I need to have sufficient food for my well being"

I roll my eyes.

"If you grow any bigger, you will scare off all the people who crosses your path" I try to pull it from under his hand.

Baba appears out of nowhere and lifts the whole pancake easily from our hands.

"I deserve this more than anyone in this room" he says taking a bite.

"Oh yeah?" mama asks placing her hands on her hips and narrowing her eyes playfully.

"I meant the both of us" baba says quickly and puts a piece of it in mama's mouth.

Me and Usmaan share unamused glances and giggle quietly, taking the dishes to put in the sink.

(◍•ᴗ•◍)

I turn to the other side of the bed when I feel sprinkles of water on my face.

Why the hell is it raining in my bedroom??

Wait!! Raining in my bedroom!!

I sit up confusedly rubbing the sleep off my face when I hear familiar chuckles near me.

"What are you guys doing in my house at this hour?" I ask both Mariam and Alina who are now plopped down on the edge of my bed still snickering.

"One" Alina says showing her index finger.

"We can be at your house whenever we want"

"And two" now Mariam says pointedly

"It's almost afternoon so I think it's a perfectly appropriate time"

"I guess I established that in my first answer that we could be here anytime we want" Alina says turning toward Mariam.

"Yeah, I know you did. I just wanted to add something on my own" Mariam replies sheepishly.

"You guys are crazy now move out of my bed and let me freshen up" I say trying to stand up.

Alina gasps dramatically "We came early to suprise you and you didn't even give us a fake surprised reaction to make us happy" she pouts.

"I guess I would react to this surprise in a better way when I'm not having an emergency to use the toilet" I say getting up and going to the bathroom.

"Eww Maira, you didn't have to be so descriptive about everything" Alina shouts from the room.

I laugh loudly at her my best friend's antics.

"Come on Alina, wake up already" I say pulling the comforter off her as Mariam shakes her awake.

"You guys, how can you be up so early? We literally slept after fajr" Alina groan pulling back her comforter.

It's been two days since these guys have come home and we have bought a wedding dress for me. It's a beautiful outfit if I say so myself. A long pearl white gown with a floor length cape upon it and both are embedded with delicate pearls. And of course a pearl white hijab and a detachable niqab of the same color.

"Alina we are having a girls day out today if you have forgotten" Mariam speaks cutting me out of my trance.

"It can start a bit later" Alina mumbles out through the comforter.

"No it can't, Usman is dropping us and he will have to leave in an hour" Mariam explains

"Who is dropping us?" Alina asks peeking through the blanket.

Mariam rolls her eyes "I'm sure that's not the only part which you heard"

Alina snickers and sits up "Yeah but that did it!! See, I am awake now."

"Girls hurry up! Usman is ready to leave." Mama comes and places the tray of breakfast on the small table near the couch.

"Shukran mama and we'll be there in 15 mins"

"Barakallahu feeki, okay I'll let him know"

"Do not eat up my breakfast too" Alina yells as she locks the bathroom door.

"We sure will" Mariam calls out and we both chuckle.

We are apparently going out today as Mariam says that we didn't have any alone time though we are staying up just chatting almost half of the night since the day they've come. I also have to purchase some accessories to go on the dress which we bought earlier--

"Okay guys we are good to go" Alina says faking a bold accent.

All of us put on our niqabs and Mariam grabs a jacket because she feels extra cold today.

"I literally feel like a chauffeur. Why don't anyone of you come and sit in the passenger seat?" Usman asks as he puts his seat-belt on.

Me and Alina nudge Mariam who is sitting in the between of us.

"Shut up" she mutters shoving our arms away.

"You basically are our chauffeur for today" I say looking at Usman.

"Say that again and you will be out of the car that instant" Usman threatens causing us to laugh.

He smiles lightly looking in the rear view mirror. I raise an eyebrow when I look at the direction he is looking at. Mariam's laughing figure. And he says that I am the delusional one.

Usman drops us off at a mall and we quickly grab our coffees from the coffee shop at the entrance to keep our day going.

And hence, our girl's day out goes by skimming through every product in almost all the shops of the mall, playing all sorts of games in the 'game zone' and finally filling our tired and empty bellies with lots and lots of food.

(◍•ᴗ•◍)

I close the Quran and keep it in its prescribed place. It's almost breakfast time and Alina is in the bathroom taking a shower while Mariam is downstairs helping mama with the breakfast. And I am having an anxious attack from the time I've woken up.

What else is been expected from a person who is having her nikah today?

Yes! It's Friday and the nikah will take place in the mosque after the Dhur prayer.

"You are not leaving the room today, are you?" Alina comes out and tying her hijab over her now dried hair.

I just shake my head and she sighs.

"What? You cannot blame okay. You guys should've gotten married before me so that I would know how to act now." I rant sitting down on the bed.

"Maira you can--"

She is cut by Mariam who enters the room calling down for breakfast.

"I guess I'll just have it here" I say unsurely.

"Maira" Mariam and Alina both warn together.

"I promise I'll be ok having my breakfast in here"

They just let out a long breath and leave the room.

"Maira" Usman calls out from the door after a while knocking it twice

.

"Yes come in"

"You're not coming down?" He asks getting in and closing the door all the while balancing a tray of food in his hand.

"No, I thought it would be better to just have my breakfast alone"

"And, why so?"

I shrug and take the tray from his hand. He sits down on the couch and serves the food on the plate.

"You are not going down too?" I ask confusedly.

"Your friends are having their breakfast with mama and besides I thought you would need a shoulder to cry on"

"Oh how generous of you" I roll my eyes and say sarcastically.

"And... we got back your normal self" he states giving me a plate.

He speaks again when he didn't get any reaction from "Oh come on little sister cheer up, it's your nikah"

"You are not helping brother"

"It is ok to feel this way Maira, instead it would've been quiet a problem if you had felt normal" I nod releasing a light breath. He drapes his arm around my shoulder and comforts me "Now let's have our food and get the day started"

My day had started long before fajr, though I had slept only after midnight yesterday. So I had prayed tahajjud and taken a shower before fajr itself.

"Did Adam's parents or his sister talk to you?" Usman asks munching down the toast.

"No they didn't. Why?"

He shook his "Adam was asking about the Mehr a few days back when we met at the mosque"

"Oh" I couldn't help the anxiousness rise inside me after hearing his name.

Usman leaves after he finishes his breakfast and leaves the room just when Alina and Mariam enter.

"You guys better be ready in less than an hour" mama says walking in behind them.

Alina fake gasps "Aunty we have to get the bride ready and her two very own best-friends in an hour?"

"Ignore her aunty we'll be ready before you even know it" Mariam brushes off Alina.

Mama smiles nodding her head and then looks at me in the eye as though trying to tell me something and then leaves, closing the door behind her.

"Yeah! so let's start" Alina exclaims rubbing her palms together.

Mariam rolls her eyes and I chuckle slightly.

(⦿•‿•⦿)

"Okay okay final touch ups" Alina says making me face her.

"Alina it is done when we will leave for the mosque" Mariam says fixing her hijab in the mirror above me.

"Yeah and you have literally just now finished doing my makeover" I agree with Mariam.

Alina rolls her eyes "Okay you two!"

"And you are not supposed to move around much" she adds pointing her finger at me.

"And why is that?" I raise an eyebrow.

"Because you will ruin your dress" she says like it's an obvious thing.

"Dude you better finish getting ready yourself up before aunty comes up to call us" Mariam reminds her.

We all are almost ready to go just like how Mariam promised mama. In just an hour or maybe even less we are done with our Dhur salahs, getting dressed up and doing our makeovers.

And just on cue mama comes in knocking on the door "I hope you are all ready girls?"

"Just as promised aunty" Mariam exclaims still fixing her hijab. This girl is never really satisfied with her hijab.

"Okay then we'll be downstairs, yeah?" Alina asks pulling up her niqab and grabs Mariam's hands as Mariam herself pulls up her niqab.

Mama nods towards them smiling politely.

"You look absolutely beautiful honey" she says turning towards me and placing her palms on my cheeks.

"You look prettier mama" I reply gulping down the lump forming in my throat.

"I cannot believe that you are being wedded already" she says blinking away her tears.

"Me neither" I chuckle softly and she pulls me into a hug, her arms draping around me securely.

"Can I come in?" we hear baba from outside the door.

"And me too?" Usman adds.

Mama laughs slightly and calls them in.

"Now, do you see that baba? A family hug without the men of the house." Usman complains putting his arms around me and mama while baba hugs us from the other side.

"We are going to miss you dumb-head"

"For the hundredth time am not leaving the house yet" I exclaim

"Oh right, my bad" he feigns disappointment.

"Usman" both mama and baba warns.

"Yeah yeah I see that it's her day today" he says and huffs.

We all laugh as we pull away and mama takes my hand into hers and leads us outside to the car. Only the immediate relatives of mine are invited to the nikah and almost all of them will directly be there in the mosque. So its just my family, Mariam and Alina. Both of them climb in the back seats of the car while me and Usman sits in the middle seats and mama sits with baba in the passenger seat.

"Have you decided about the Mehr?" Usman whispers in my ear.

I nod, "I've told mama about it."

"Okay."

I lay my head on his shoulder while I realize the gravity of the event which is going to be taken place in less than an hour. Alhamdulillah that Allah has made me reach this point of my life and I cannot thank Him enough for the blessings he is bestowed upon me. I make an instant pray, asking Him to give me enough strength and patience for everything which is to come further.

Usman extends his hand out once he gets out of the car. He squeezes my hand reassuringly while nodding his head. Mama comes in beside me and we go towards the mosque saying a quick Bismillah.

"Assalamualaikum" Adam's mom says approaching us.

"Walaikumasslam" I reply quietly while the others reply too.

"Let us first go in the room across before we proceed with the nikah ceremony." She says pointing to a corner covered with curtains.

Usman lets go off my hand and kisses my forehead while whispering "Fee amaanillah (Be with the safety of Allah)" in my ear.

"I wanted to talk to you about something, child" Adam's mom tells me quietly once mama and my friends leave to tend to our relatives who have arrived in the back garden of the masjid.

My heartbeat takes a quicker pace as I look back at Aisha who is giving me a concerned and a reassuring look.

I nod my head silently asking Adam's mom to continue with what she wants to say.

She clears her throat and begins "Adam told me about the actual reason why Aisha brought out the proposal for you and I am truly sorry for the way he invaded your privacy on that day at your college event. He might've already apologized for that but I don't want you to be forced into entering this relationship out of the fear of Adam telling this to us."

I shake my head trying to find appropriate words "You don't have to apologize for anything aunty and I'm surely not forced into this relationship. I believe that Adam would never do anything which would be a means of fear to me" I say looking down and make mental note to smack myself later for the little statement of mine at the end.

"Are you noticing the trust which she have in Adam already mama?" Aisha asks smirking mischievously.

"I am glad she does and start calling me mama already" she said pointedly towards me.

I smile and nod.

"I'll go check if everything is ready outside" she says leaving me and Aisha.

I sigh audibly and Aisha lets out a relieved breathe too.

"Adam didn't want anything to be hidden about you and him. He just wanted to be in the clear before the Nikah." She explains.

Mama, Mariam and my naanu (grandmother) come in before I could reply. Naanu greets me with a hug and a kiss on my cheek "My little grown up girl" she says.

"Everything is ready outside and people are waiting for the bride" Alina says peeking through the curtain.

Mama comes beside me and Mariam comes to hold my hand on the other side as we head out.

I feel my hands begin to sweat and my heart pounds rapidly. Keeping my eyes lowered to the ground I walk further and feel the hall go silent.

It is finally happening!

I think I will pass out from the way my heart quickens even faster now. I am placed on a couch across from that of a couch on which there are men sitting, probably Adam and someone else. Mama sits besides me while naanu sits on the other side.

The Imam then starts the ceremony with a 'Bismillahirahmaan nir-raheem' and says the nikah pledge in Arabic. He asks me and Adam to repeat it which we do. The nikah papers are then passed to me, I sign and Adam signs them after me. My heart flutters when I realize that Allah has bestowed this blessing of unconditional love and I have successfully fulfilled half of my religion.

The people around congratulate us both and mama hugs me from the side and kisses my forehead. I lift my eyes nervously and look at Adam to see him hugging his father. His gaze falls upon me and he smiles widely.

A tender, genuine and the most beautiful smile I have ever seen. I smile back at him, but I am not quite sure that he actually saw me smiling because of my niqab.

Baba and Usman comes beside me and congratulate giving a loving hug. My eyes fall back to the blue-grey eyes shielded with the same vintage glass which draws my attention all over again.

Mariam, Alina, Amina and Zainab pull me towards the end of the stage interrupting my stare.

"I am so happy for you"

"Congratulations Maira"

"I can't believe that you are married"

"It has finally happened"

All four of them gush and hug me.

I smile at them as mama comes to tell us that we are leaving to our place. We are apparently having a small dinner gathering for all the guests who have come today. Mariam stays with me while the others go with mama to call the others.

"You finally got your other half, huh?" she asks grinning.

"Seems like it" I reply looking down.

"Aisha where were you?" Mariam asks Aisha who approaches us with a wide smile.

"I was just there with my brother making sure he doesn't pass out with the amount of happiness around him"

"Which reminds me that he is coming here" she adds and I look up at her words.

I quickly lower my eyes when I see Adam and Usman coming towards us.

"Assalamualaikum ladies" Usman says standing beside me.

We all mumble a reply and I grasp Mariam's hand when I see Adam stand directly in front of me. My heart beats rapidly in my chest and my hold on Mariam's hand tightens.

"Assalamualaikum" his deep and husky yet a gentle voice say.

I fail to reply due to my anxiousness and the others reply just how they did to Usman.

Mariam forcefully removes her hand from mine and speaks "So...we will leave it to you two then"

"I don't think you would need a chaperone now" Aisha whispers and winks at me.

Usman doesn't budge from his position instead he puts a protective arm around my shoulders. Mariam looks at him and sighs "Usman come on"

He looks down at me asking if I would be ok. I nod, reassuringly and he reluctantly leaves me, Aisha walks towards them too leaving me and Adam alone.

"Assalamualaikum" he says again causing my nervousness to come back.

"Walaikumasslam" I reply and cringe internally at how squeaky my voice sounded.

"Congratulations Mrs. Adam Abdullah" I blush at his words and a smile seems to be fixed on my face.

"Congratulations to you too" I say looking up at him for the first time in a while. He is wearing a plain white keffiyeh with a black ring on it and one end of it is tucked behind.

"Thank you for becoming my other half" my heart flutters by his words.

"I still cannot believe that I can actually call you my lawfully wedded wife" he smiles more widely if that's even possible.

He leans in to kiss my forehead and holds my hands gently. My body quivers with the closeness and I look down at our joined hands.

"I would love to see the blush on your cheeks right now" he says and my cheeks heat up even more.

"Sorry to disturb you two love birds but we really have to get going" Alina interrupts us and I slightly pull away, Adam leaves one of my hand but intertwines my other hand with his'.

I look up at his face and he winks at me with his already smiling face. I tighten my grip on his hand to prevent myself from swooning from that handsome wink. He smirks when he notices my reaction and Alina comes to my other side and lead us to the outside of the mosque before I could embarrass myself further.

(◍•ᴗ•◍)

"What if I don't match up to his expectations?" I ask wriggling my hands together nervously.

"You already are more than his expectations, he made that clear when he acted all lovey-dovey with you in the mosque" Alina says sitting on the bed next to me.

I scoff and discreetly try cover the blush forming on my cheeks.

"Why should I even have to uncover my face in front of him?" I ask sighing.

"He is your husband if you have forgotten" Mariam reminds sarcastically.

"Girls Adam is coming up here" mama says coming up to the door and my nerves spike up.

It has been a while since we have returned from the mosque and me and all the girls have directly come to my room. Now I am supposed to meet Adam without my niqab, alone!

May Allah give me the strength to not to faint out of the nervousness.

"Best of luck okay and don't forget to give the present which you have bought for him." Mariam and Alina hug me comfortingly and leave with all the others.

I stand near my bed turning my back towards the door when I hear a knock.

I send a quick prayer to Allah and ask the person on the door to come in. I hear soft footsteps and the sound of the closing door.

"Salaam" he says softly. I contemplate on turning back or answering but before I could do anything he speaks again "Maira" my heart almost leaps out of my chest at how beautifully my name rolls out of his lips.

I inhale a long breathe and turn around "Walaikumassalam" I reply looking up at his flustered face.

I wish I could actually read minds to know what thoughts are going on in his head.

"You look gorgeous, stunning and absolutely beautiful" he exclaims in a raspy voice taking a step forward with each of his words until he is just in front of me towering my slightly short figure.

"You don't have to say anything which you don't mean, just out of courtesy" I say looking up at his eyes.

Those blue-grey eyes.

He shakes his head chuckling softly "I mean every single word which I've spoken to you until now"

"And you are just so much more amazing than what I had imagined" he adds leaning a bit closer and I gulp down at our proximity.

"How would you know that it is the same niqabi girl with whom you had only a single encounter and that too very long back?" I ask raising an eyebrow.

He laughs again, a quiet and soft laugh, and brings one of his hands to my right cheek gently caressing it "I could never forget these hazel eyes sweetheart and you actually think that I wouldn't be able to recognize your voice, my ears have it recorded when they heard it for the first time." My heartbeat accelerates with every word, and his gentle strokes on my cheek only add on to my rapid heart.

"I had felt so blessed when I saw you sign our nikah papers and now when I look at you I feel ecstatic. I cannot thank Allah enough for what He has bestowed upon me." He continues and my heart swells with happiness and love for the person in front of me.

I smile "I feel the equal amount of happiness when I see what Allah has chosen for me too" I say still gazing in his eyes.

"I love you for the sake of Allah Maira" he says with an intake of breathe.

"I love you for the sake of Allah Adam" I reply with the same smile lingering on my face.

His eyes widen for a moment "You do?" he asks bewildered.

I roll my eyes at his oblivious state "Of course I do, then why would I have gotten married to you in the first place."

"Right" he says relaxing slightly.

"Shukran Zawjati (my wife) for becoming the most beautiful blessing of my life" he says leaning forward and placing his lips on mine.

Shukran Ya Rab-al-Alameen!

Chapter-12: My wife, Zawjati.

A DAM

Alhamdulillah!

It is what that I have been saying ever since we signed the nikah papers, ever since we uttered those words at our nikah and ever since I saw her.

She is beautiful.

I had obviously tried to picture her face before but what I actually saw was just extraordinary. Wallahi! I couldn't take my eyes off her and I sure as heck didn't want to leave her there back and come home.

Why do we even have to wait till the Walima to move in together?

Patience Adam! Patience!

"Brother Mama is calling you down, they will be here any minute" Aisha says through the door.

I release a long breathe and follow her down. Mama has invited Maira and everyone else for dinner today and they are yet to come. We left their home yesterday soon after dinner and I just got to say a goodbye to her that too in front of her friends.

She is my wife now for Allah's sake.

A little privacy for the newly wedded wouldn't hurt anyone right? Heck at-least a goodbye kiss. Okay-okay that might be a bit too much to ask.

"Your smile doesn't seem to stop forming since the nikah, hmm?" baba asks coming in the living room.

I scratch the back of my neck and bite my inner lip to stop myself from smiling any wider.

The bell rings just as baba sits on the couch across mine. I quickly stand up smoothing my jeans and the flannel shirt and hurry towards the door to unlock it.

Mama comes behind me and Aisha joins, snickering at my impatience. I open the door to find Baba and Mama- Yes I started calling them that at the dinner yesterday and it actually feels good to know that you now have two set of people whom you can call parents Alhamdulillah.

"Assalamualaikum wa rahmatullahi wa barakatuhu" he greets all of us and comes forward to hug me.

"Walaikumasslam wa rahmatullahi wa barakatuhu" we all reply simultaneously and I look behind them for any traces of my very own wife.

The word literally gives me a sense of delight and comfort.

"She is coming with Usman, he had some things to finish before he leaves so they'll be here in a while" Mama (her mama) says noticing my wandering eyes.

I clear my throat and nod, slightly embarrassed and disappointed at waiting for my wife again.

I cannot stop myself from saying that word every time I want to mention her.

My wife, Zawjati.

I awkwardly sit with baba and baba (her baba) while they talk about random things when the bell rings again, I stand up immediately and go towards the door. Baba laughs loudly as I accidentally trip on the small table placed in the middle of the living room.

Stupid impatience.

I intake an anticipated breathe and open the door. Smiling widely only for it to falter when I see Yusuf, Aisha's husband. Seriously! Who has even invited him here?

"Salaam" Aisha says coming from beside me and hugging him.

"Oh, did I forget to mention that he is joining us too?" she asks smirking.

I am sure she is well aware of my impatience.

Ughh why is everyone arriving except for my wife?

Yusuf comes in saying salaam and goes to sit with the other men in the room. I lock the door and turn to go towards the room and just then I hear a car drive through our driveway.

Oh Allah please let this be her.

I wait for few moments and then unlock the door to see a struggling Maira whose abaya seems to have gotten stuck in the car. She finally frees herself from the trouble and lean in the car to take two small boxes of Allah knows what. I instinctively take a step forward to help her out but her brother comes to her side and insists on taking those boxes from her. She shakes her head and gives him only one of those boxes. She glares at him hard when he tries to take the other box too. I smile at her kind gestures. My woman. My wife.

They come towards the door and instantly notice my presence there. Maira- my wife looks down shyly while Usman smiles at me and bumps his shoulder with hers causing her to glare at him again.

"Assalamualaikum" I say once they are exactly in front of me.

"Walaikumasslam" They say together and Usman comes forward to hug me awkwardly with the box in one of his hand.

Do I get to hug my wife too? Of course I should get.

Usman notices our hesitance and leaves the two of us taking the box from Maira's hands.

I clear my throat and smile at her once she looks at me.

Those eyes.

"How have you been?" I ask, inching towards her to hold her hand.

"Alhamdulillah, how about you?"

"Alhamdulillah, except for the part where I had been impatiently waiting for my wife to arrive." I say finally holding her soft hands. She chuckles softly and looks down.

"Usman had some errands to run that is the reason we were a bit late"

I nod "Mama told me about it" she looks at me suddenly at the mention of her mama, her eyes showing a sense of appreciation and admiration.

Oh the things I would to see that look.

"I am glad to hear you call her that" she says her eyes truly showing the smile on her face which I am unable to see.

"I would be glad if I---"

"Oh Maira, when did you arrive?" Aisha comes in cutting me.

"Just a little while back" Maira replies trying to take my hand off hers.

I am not letting her go. Not today. She is my wife for Allah's sake man.

"Okay come on in. I'll show you around" Aisha grabs her other hand.

"I'll do it" I speak before she could take away my wife.

"Oh come on Adam, don't be so clingy" she says removing my hand from hers and laughing at my scowling face.

They walk away and Maira looks back at me before turning in the dining room and I am very sure that she is smiling under her niqab.

My wife.

(◍•ᴗ•◍)

"When is your college resuming again?" Usman asks from beside me on the dining table. He has been quite the interrogator since he has stepped inside. Yusuf however has been turning in and out in our conversations every now and then.

"From Monday" I reply putting a morsel of food in my mouth.

"Maira's college is starting from the same day too right?" baba asks now joining in our conversation.

"Yes it is"

"Yes"

I and Usman both reply at the same time. I look over at him to see him looking back at me with his brows raised. I clear my throat and look down at my plate, heat crawling up my neck.

Of course I know things about my wife!

Aisha comes in taking the used plates to the kitchen. I and Yusuf follow taking few dishes ourselves.

"Take Maira for a house tour Adam" Aisha says placing the plates on the counter.

I nod slightly, internally bursting with joy at having my wife to myself for once.

"Wait here, I'll go get her" she goes back to the lawn where the ladies are seated.

Yusuf leaves the kitchen patting my back and I nervously lean my back on the kitchen counter.

Soft giggles and footsteps come towards the kitchen and I straighten myself. "Assalamualaikum" Maira says through her niqab. My smile falters a little bit when I don't see her face.

"Walaikumasslam"

"Okay I'll leave it to you two then" Aisha says turning her back and leaving the kitchen. "Have fun" she calls back.

"Uhh, I'll show you around then?" I say, more like question her.

She nods her head silently humming a response.

I walk towards the stairs with her following closely behind me. I clear my throat in a fail attempt to strike up a conversation.

"So all set for the college on Monday?" Seriously Adam?? You finally get your wife to yourself and the first thing you ask is about college?

I seriously need this counseling session where I learn to speak appropriately with my wife.

"Pretty much, how about you?" she questions glancing towards me and holding the railings of the stairs.

"Pretty much" I smile nodding slightly.

I need a revision on my vocabulary.

She chuckles softly shaking her head.

I show her around the house. Mama and baba's room, Aisha's room, the guest room and the terrace. The look of adoration in her eyes told me that she loves everything of what she has seen. I wonder what she will say when she sees our room. She is more comfortable now from the time we started this little house tour. Its apparent in her posture, she seems more relaxed, free and...content.

Alhamdulillah.

"Either you didn't show me your room yet or you just belong to the couch in the living room." She states with a playful glint in her voice.

Remember about her feeling comfortable? Well it is evident.

"Our room and yes I do have a room." I say the last part playfully narrowing my eyes at her.

She laughs, an actual laugh.

And it's incredible.

"Very well then, lead the way" she says motioning her hand towards the terrace door. I quickly grab hold of that hand and give her a satisfactory smile.

"This is our room" I say opening the door to the last room in the hallway. She gets in and I close the door behind us already planning to spend a little extra time here.

"Hmm, impressive." Maira nods to herself appreciatively. "It is beautiful and really...clean" she trails off.

Now do I tell her that I literally begged Aisha to clean my room earlier today?

"I asked Aisha to do it today." I couldn't question myself anymore when it comes to Maira. I have this weird urge to say everything and anything to her and listen to everything which she has to say to me. To know that there is a person who is especially made for you to listen to, to hold, to keep and to love is exceptional. And to know that Maira is that person for me is beyond amazing. I silently pray to Allah to make me the person with whom she would feel exactly the same way like how I feel with her. Grateful, Undeniably grateful.

"You anyway didn't strike me as a 'keeping my room clean' type of person" she says mischievously.

I raise my eyebrows "Oh yeah, what type of person did I strike you as then?"

She shrugs lowering her niqab and eyeing the door cautiously. My heart escalates when I realize how much she is starting to feel comfortable around me in such a short span of time.

"If anyone comes here, they would knock before entering" I say understanding her hesitance.

She smiles visibly relaxing at my words. "I am glad to see that you trust me enough to be this comfortable" I voice out my thoughts pointing to her niqab.

"I am"

"And I have been in desperate need of some direct air" she adds fanning herself with her hands.

"And I have been in desperate need of seeing your face"

She turns completely red at my remark. Well I am not lying though.. I have been wanting to see her face ever since she entered our house. I just cannot get over at how incredibly beautiful she looks.

"I have something to give you" she says clearing her throat and skill-fully changing the course of the conversation.

"I do too" I wanted to give her the wedding gift soon after the nikah but I didn't get enough time yesterday and it also completely got out of my mind.

"Yeah?" she asks raising her eyebrows.

I nod and ask her to go first. She digs out a black box out of her handbag and hands it to me. An all black leather band watch comes into my view as I open the box. I slide my fingers over the leather bands and smile at her.

"JazakAllahu Khairan sweetheart"

She chuckles softly her cheeks tinting a deep shade of red. "Your sudden endearments startle me"

"Well get used to it, Zawjati" I smirk and open the bedside drawer to take her gift out.

I open the box myself, taking out the platinum ring and placing the empty box back on the bed.

"Allow me" I gently grab her right hand and slide the ring in one of her fingers. She smiles adoringly at the ring and glances at me, the smile getting wider.

"The stone is the color of your eyes" she exclaims in a charming voice.

"Is it? I didn't know that you have noticed the color of my eyes" I tease going a bit closer to her and taking her hand back in mine.

Yes, I like holding her.

"Of course I did-- wait you are teasing me" she realizes and whines.

"Am I now, sweetheart?" I ask placing the other hand on her waist and leaning my forehead on hers.

"Stop with the endearments Adam" she blushes looking down.

"I've always wanted to call you with nicknames as many as I can, love."

"Then it's only fair if I call you with one." She states.

"But I love how my name rolls out of your lips." I say gazing at her hazel eyes.

"Then Adam it is" she concludes. I gaze a little longer in her eyes and drop my forehead on her shoulder. "I love you Maira and I cannot wait to spend my entire life with you."

"I love you too Adam and I cannot wait to spend my life with you in this world and in Jannah inshaAllah"

"InshaAllah"

Chapter-13: Say it.

M AIRA

"Okay mama Assalamualaikum, I'm leaving" I call back to mama struggling to put my shoes from one hand and opening the door with the other. Mama replies back as I am locking the door behind me and hopping in the passenger seat of Usman's car.

"Ahh finally" he says as he turns on the car.

Yes I am late and like really late, I don't even know if I can make it to my first class today and the traffic is not helping. Apparently, I woke up late in spite of mama coming and waking me up five whole times but I couldn't help being that sleepy when I literary slept after fajr. I was awake the whole night and there is a certain vintage glass guy who is to be blamed for occupying my head with his thoughts and heart with these newly found emotions towards him. His words from the time at his house have still been ringing in my ears. And I couldn't seem to shake of the feeling of his actions from that day. A soft smile appears on my face as I caress the grey-blue stone on my finger which is yet to be accustomed to my hand.

"If you are done with gazing at that ring on your finger then you can get out of the car respectfully" Usman says tapping my shoulder with a flat look.

"We've arrived?" I turn to look at the empty entrance of the college.

I have missed my first class.

"Yes, now come on get going already" he hurries.

"Okay! Okay! I'm going" I yell out as I open the door.

I go to the cafeteria to wait till it's time for the second class. There are literally very few to no one around the hallways and its way too silent so when my phone rings in my bag, the voice travels in the whole cafeteria. I quickly pick it up to see Aisha calling me.

"Heyy Assalamualaikum" Aisha's cheerful voice come through the speaker and I furrow my brows. She is obviously not in her class.

"Walaikumassalam"

"Are you not in class?" I add.

"Are you not in class?" she asks back and I roll my eyes at her words "I just now reached the campus...Woke up late"

"What about you?" I asked.

"We also have just reached the college...and I was not the person who woke up late" I furrow my brows at her response. "We?"

"Yup, I had to wait the whole thirty minutes for your lazy husband to get ready. Apparently it was him who woke up late" I bite my lip from smiling any wider at her choice of words.

"Now to think about it, I wonder how it is such a co-incidence..." she drawls.

"Aisha, stop it already" a voice whom I've come to admire grumbles behind her.

"Okay tell me where you are?" she asks hurriedly.

"Cafeteria"

"Cool, we'll be there in a minute" she hangs up before I could say anything else.

I go to the counter to grab a coffee when I hear set of footsteps in the almost empty area.

"Assalamualaikum" Aisha comes in giving me a cheery hug. My heart unconsciously starts beating a bit faster thinking about just seeing the person who has been occupying my thoughts lately.

"Walaikumassalam, will you guys have coffee? I was just getting one for myself" I ask still not removing my gaze from her.

"Of course, I'll get it" she moves to go further towards the counter leaving me of no choice than to greet her brother.

I gulp down nervously and look up at Adam who is standing just a few feet apart, a soft smile on his lips and head quiet slightly tilted.

"Assalamualaikum" I start and he smiles a bit wider coming right in front of me.

"Walaikumassalam" he says and comes a bit closer, bringing his face dangerously close to my covered one.

"I was waiting for my wife to finally notice me" he whispers near my ear and my heart which was already racing increases its pace, if only that was possible.

He looks back at me with the same smile but slightly smirking and leans in to kiss my forehead which is clad with my hijab and niqab.

I silently thank Allah for the niqab which is helping in covering my flustered face.

"Okay guys, here... your coffees" Aisha comes handing us our cups.

We go to sit in one of the chairs placed near the windows.

"So, how have you been feeling since the Nikah?" she asks me wiggling her eyebrows mischievously.

"She has been going on with this since the day you came to our place" Adam says with an eye roll.

I laugh quietly at his annoyed expression and look back at Aisha "Happy" I reply discreetly looking at a smiling Adam.

"Happy? That's it I was obviously expecting a bit more than just a word" she whines. "At least your response is better than this jerk here" she says playfully shoving Adam's shoulder.

I perk up at her words "Why? what was his response?' I ask, trying not to sound that desperate.

"Desperate much?" she asks. Okay well I did sound desperate. I shrug and lift my niqab slightly to take a sip of my coffee trying to not feel completely embarrassed at my stupid curiousness.

"He just said that 'he doesn't seem to be wanting to tell me' his words not mine." She glares at him causing him to chuckle and roll his eyes again. I myself slightly chuckle at her childishness when her phone starts ringing in her bag.

"Oh I guess I'll get going, it's my friend probably calling me for the class. Ma'salaam" she waves her hand grabbing her bag and then leaving.

"Finally" Adam lets a long sigh.

"Why should there always be someone when I just want my wife to myself?" He exasperates.

"You are just exaggerating now" I say laughing lightly.

He raises his brows, leaning on the table towards me keeping his gaze locked on my eyes. "I was literally dying to meet you from yesterday and now you're telling me that I am exaggerating sweetheart?" he asks quietly, feigning hurt. My stomach does these stupid flips at his quiet voice.

"Tell me what kept you awake the whole night that got you late for college?" he asks again before I could speak anything.

"I could ask the same thing to you" I ask tilting my head slightly.

"Oh that will be an easy answer... it were all the thoughts of you which kept me awake last night" he winks.

He winks. Oh my Allah!! That would be the most gorgeous thing I've ever seen!! Snap out of it Maira!!!

"And... by the looks of your eyes I can say that yours was the same case, wasn't it?" he whispers.

"Uhh. I guess I'll have to get going before I get late to the class again" I say clearing my throat and standing up.

What the hell am I supposed to do in situations like these?

He places his hand firmly on my own and stops me from taking my bag.

"I love you sweetheart" he says smiling beautifully.

I smile too though I am not sure if he can sense it.

"Come on say it, I have been waiting to hear my name from you again" he says hurriedly.

I smile internally at what I am about to say "Maybe I would, if I wouldn't have been getting late for the class" I say with a hint of mischief in my voice.

"Now my love, I am not leaving you until you say it" he says standing up and coming towards me.

"Ma'salaam" I say as I run away from him and towards my class.

(◍•ᴗ•◍)

"Now quit daydreaming and focus" Amina snaps her fingers from beside me and pointed towards Mr. Collins who was writing a code on the board.

"I wasn't" I whine "And my complete focus was in there" I add now pointing to the board myself.

Amina rolls her eyes and begins to say something when Zainab cuts her off "Guys we all will be kicked out if you both don't stop now" she hisses.

"Tell that to her" I say narrowing my eyes at Amina.

"Okay class, study the codes for the next class. Have a great day" Mr. Collins says as he picks his stuff and then dismisses the class.

"That's it for the day right?" Amina asks packing her bag.

"Yup Alhamdulillah" Zainab replies.

"It feels like we haven't gotten out of this class for like forever" I sigh and lean my head on the desk.

"Yeah because you were too scared to face Adam again"

"And let me add that he is your dear husband" Zainab pipes in our conversation.

"I wasn't scared, I was just little bit nervous" I said silently thanking Allah for the niqab which efficiently covers my reddening cheeks.

"Same thing" Amina rolls her eyes.

By the time Amina and Zainab wear their abayas the whole class is emptied. It is not unusual, we mostly are always the last one to exit our class.

"Our classes start late tomorrow" Zainab reminds.

Amina nods "But we'll still come a bit early, we'll hang around or something"

I shrug and nod my head in affirmative.

Just as we step out of the class and into the hallway, we see a tall figure leaning on the side of the wall.

Which so happens to be Adam!!

I gulp down the nervousness and tighten my hold on Amina's hand and proceed to go with them to the side of the hallway, while Amina and Zainab knowingly slow their pace.

What is it with these girls now?

"Maira" he calls out loud enough for us to hear although there is mostly no one in this hallway.

I feel my heart start to beat faster and I'm not able to figure out why I am having this feeling even after having so many conversations with him.

I inhale and exhale deeply before turning around to face him. Amina discreetly tries to remove her hand from mine while I tighten it.

Why on earth am I nervous to talk to my own husband?

"Uhh we'll just be downstairs waiting for you alright?" Amina says removing my hand completely out of hers now. I glare at her and turn back again to look at Adam. He is wearing a charcoal colored hoodie and black jeans paired with black sneakers.

He takes slow steps towards me and look behind me probably to make sure that my friends were gone. "Stop trying to run away from your own husband, darling." he says taking my right hand in his and gently stroking the back of my palm with his hand.

"I wasn't running away from you" I lie.

Astaghfirullah!

"Of course you weren't" he says smirking.

I roll my eyes from him and look at the outside view of the building. He chuckles softly and follows my gaze.

"I was hoping I could drop you off at your place today?" he asks hesitantly.

"Your classes are done?" I ask back.

"Is that a yes?" he asks again.

"Stop asking question to my questions" I say as a soft smile comes up to my lips.

"You were the one who started it" he says childishly.

"Anyway, so lets go" he puts his hand forward for me to grab it.

I take hold of his hand and fiddle with my phone to call my brother to inform him.

"Don't worry about that I've already asked your brother about it" he says looking at me.

"You did?"

"I didn't expect you to ask him anything like that after the nikah you know because we are halal and everything now..." I trail off.

"He might come off as a bit intimidating and yes we are halal" he squeezes my hand and places a soft kiss on my niqab clad cheeks before continuing "but he is still your brother and I respect that" my heart soars in admiration for this guy whom I have come to love and proud to call my husband.

"Thanks" I say looking at him with a smile hoping he would be able to feel it from my eyes. He pinches my cheeks slightly and smiles mischievously "You can always return the gesture by saying those few words which I am dying to hear since morning" he exasperates.

"Oh I am not quite sure what those words were" I tease him.

"Do I have to remind you sweetheart?" he asks as his hands go up to my waist and he starts tickling.

"Adam stop! I will fall off the stairs" I shriek trying to balance my foot on the stairs.

"I am here to catch you my love" he says as he continues with his childish actions.

"Aww how cheesy..." I say, finally pushing him off me and running down the stairs.

(◍•ᴗ•◍)

He shuts off the engine as we reach in the driveway of my place and turns toward me keeping the doors closed.

"I am yet to see your face today" he says expectantly.

I smile and lower my niqab. His smile grows even wider as he leans in to place a kiss on my cheeks now.

"I love you so really much sweetheart" he whispers near my ear and strokes the other cheek with his hand.

I stay silent for a moment or two anticipating his next words. "Come on now, say it already" he whines placing his forehead on my shoulder.

"I love you so really much too Mr. Adam Abdullah" I smile as he lifts his head to look at me.

"Well then until tomorrow Mrs. Adam Abdullah. Ma'salaam" he whispers again bumping my nose with his.

I am surely having a panic attack at his gestures today!!

Chapter-14: Dammit.

A DAM

"I was thinking if I could take Maira to college tomorrow... I am anyway going to the same place" I say clearing my throat nervously.

"Of course you can, son and you don't have to ask" Her baba says calmly.

"But it's fine for me to drop her. The college is just on my way. You don't have to worry yourself over that" Usman says skeptically.

I think of ways to convince him when baba speaks again "Oh come on Usman, cut this boy some slack for being Maira's husband"

Usman shrugs in response though his eyes are trained on me. Wallahi, Usman is more intimidating than his own father.

I look around the living room for my wife when I hear soft voices from across the kitchen. Apparently I had been dropping off Maira to her home for quite a few days now and today her baba spotted me out and invited me over for dinner. I was thinking I could pick Maira from her home early tomorrow and we'll get to spend sometime before our classes start but I didn't expect her brother as well to be present today.

"Adam why don't you go freshen up yourself and take some rest until dinner time" Mama says while she and Maira enter the living room.

A soft smile comes up to my life on seeing Maira again "Yeah Mama sure, I'll just go up then..." I trail off standing up and looking at Maira, silently asking her to accompany me.

"Maira go and help him out" Mama speaks looking towards Maira.

"Shukran mama" I show a grateful smile to her to which she nods her head reassuringly and smiles.

"I wonder whose characteristics your brother has" I say quiet enough for Maira to hear once we reach the stairs.

Maira looks at me with puzzled face "Your mother and your father both have a lovely aura around them but your brother scares the shit out of me" I say chuckling lightly.

"I wonder what has caused you to say this" she says mocking my previous words.

"He wouldn't let me take my own wife to the college" I whine playfully.

She chuckles "Of course he didn't"

"Okay I might slightly be acting as a hypocrite now because I am as skeptical as him with Yusuf" I reply scratching the back of my neck.

"I would never understand the protectiveness of you brothers" she shakes her head opening the door to her room.

"You act all mean with us yet you are not okay if our own husbands ask to take us out for once" she laughs.

"It's just a brother's thing I guess" I shrug.

"I'll get some clothes from Usman till you get showered" she says turning back to the door again.

"It will fit you, wouldn't it?" she continues.

"It will, but you don't have to hurry yourself out" I say grabbing her hand and stopping her from going out of the room.

She arches one of her brows at my sudden actions "The big reason as to why I stayed for dinner was because I would get more time to spend with you" I say pulling her closer to me.

"And?" she trails off looking up into my eyes.

Man I love her eyes and her short cute height and her sweet scent...oh I just love her.

Dammit. I shake my head at my thoughts smiling to myself.

"What are you thinking about?" she asks with those cute narrow eyes.

"You" I whisper back.

She rolls her eyes "I am standing right in front of you and in your arms" she points out with her eyes.

"Am I not allowed to think about you even if you are in front of me or even in my arms for that matter?" I question, mocking her in the last.

A tint of red coats on her already pink cheeks as she pushes me away "You need go shower" she says and leaves giggling softly to herself.

This woman.

(⫯•‿•⫯)

"You are undeniably plain" Maira drawls as she taps her fingers urgently on the ice cream counter.

"Oh common, vanilla is not that bad" I defend myself.

"It is obviously not, but you need to add some things on the top of it" she says in a hushed voice.

"There is no harm in trying something new then" I say with a slight smirk.

"Oh am I seeing the big Adam agreeing to get some cute toppings on his ice cream?" she teases.

"I am just agreeing to my wife" I wink and kiss her on the cheeks over her grey niqab.

"Oh please" she says trying to brush it off but I am sure on my life that she is blushing underneath it.

Just then the man comes with our ice-creams and Maira excitedly asks him to add some toppings on mine and her ice-cream. And she makes him add a lots of them.

Once we get into the car she waits patiently for my reaction to the plain vanilla ice cream which is now with toppings.

"Hmm. It does actually tastes nice" I nod taking another spoon of my ice-cream.

"I am sure you are just under rating it now. I can say by just looking at it that it tastes more than amazing." She says excitedly eyeing the cup I my hand.

I smile at her and push my cup towards her "Wanna try?"

"Only if you try mine" she demands tilting her head slightly. I nod and take her grape flavored ice-cream.

We are actually on our way back to home from college when Maira intended on stopping by an ice-cream parlor. It's all good with me if I get to spend more time with my wife.

We've been travelling to and fro college and home from many days and I am looking forward to taking her to my place someday inshaAllah. I have my final exams starting in a week or two and so does Maira and our parents are probably planning for our walima which will be in our semester break. I also have big plans for after our walima and I really hope she likes it.

"So you should come over our place sometime..." I trail off expectantly.

"Aisha would really love to see you" I continue.

"Aisha sees me everyday at college Adam" My heart does a flip listening to my name from her mouth and I embarrassingly bite my lip at the stupid reason I gave her to come home.

"Uhh... mama would love to see you too and Aisha would like to see you at home" I reply stressing at the last part of my sentence.

"Hmm. InshaAllah I will. Maybe tomorrow or Sunday."

"It's weekend anyway so InshaAllah" she continues.

"So I will come to pick you up ok? Call me when you've decided" I say immediately.

She laughs at my hurriedness "I will. I will." she says shaking her head.

(◍•ᴗ•◍)

"How did you just plan out of nowhere?" I ask her through the phone.

"It has been so long since I've seen them, so I just thought it would be nice to give them a surprise" she explains.

"Come on it's not so long. You have seen them like a month back at our nikah. And not to forget the fact that you guys have the video chats so often" I state as a matter of fact.

"And why can't they come here and meet you, it would be the same thing anyway" I add muttering the last part.

"Surprise Adam. It is a surprise. So how can they coming here would be a surprise for them?"

"But you are going to miss your college and exams are also nearing, so how can you miss classes at this point?" I ask hoping to convince her.

"Why do you seem to be more worried about my classes than me?" she asks knowingly with a smirk lacing her voice.

"You know why," I say dejectedly.

"No I don't," she states in a teasing tone.

"Maira" I drawl out with a long sigh.

"Adam" she mocks me, giggling softly.

Damn that voice... I am totally into this woman and she is asking me why I don't want her to go.

"Okay I got to go have dinner, so I'll call you later?" she asks.

"Unless you would be busy or something." she adds immediately trailing off.

"Sweetheart I don't want you to go out of the state for a few days and you think I would not want to hear your voice, even if it is for second" I exclaim.

"Okay, got it, you will be free to talk to me after a while," she says in a quite flustered voice.

"Ma'salaam" she adds.

"Ma'salaam" I reply back before she hangs up.

I fall back on my pillow with an apparent smile on my face. It is just the thought of her which fixes even my worst of worst moods. My smile drops thinking of how I would be able stay without seeing her face for five whole days. Five days. And she is just telling me now that she has planned her visit to her friends place. I wonder how so many thoughts go on in that head of hers, I mean she was just here last night having dinner with mama, baba and Aisha and today she's planning on going to surprise her friends.

Thinking back to the dinner, the smile comes back on my face at how nicely she got along with everyone yesterday, her sweet voice when she laughed with mama and Aisha and the long talks we both had in our room by the end of the day. Yesterday was just beautiful and I wish to have more of days like it in the future inshAllah.

And I am surely going to drop her off to the station tomorrow. Could surely not miss seeing her once more before she leaves now, could I?

InshaAllah.

Chapter-15: Special.

M^{AIRA}

I toss my bag next to Alina who is sitting at the back and head to the passenger seat of the car. I had just now arrived at the station to find Maryam and Alina already waiting for me. They began ranting about how they were waiting for more than half an hour for me even before greeting me properly.

I cannot really blame them though, Adam had very reluctantly let me go off to board the train. Not to mention that he literally sat with me complaining about me leaving him by himself till the announcement of the train's departure went off.

Who would have thought that The Adam Abdullah would act all soft and clingy someday?

It's so very cute to see this side Adam and what is more nice is the fact that I am one of the few people whom he have chosen to show this side of him.

I let out a silent chuckle. His clinginess is starting to rub off on me. I have just now arrived here in Canterbury and I'm missing him already.

Just then my phone starts ringing in my bag in the back seat. "Here" Alina hands it to me grunting playfully at the caller Id.

Looks like I am not the only one who is missing someone.

"Assalamualaikum" I say once I pick the call up.

"Missing me already?" I speak again before he could reply.

He chuckles from the other end "Walaikumassalam and sweetheart you would be here sleeping in front of me and I would still be missing you."

I try to laugh off his remark trying to not show him the effect of his words.

I can literally feel the heat on my cheeks and the butterflies in my stomach.

"Did I get you speechless with just my words now Zawjati?" he asks in a teasing tone.

"So uhm... why did you call?" I stutter out a response and my friends laugh beside.

Stupid people.

"Just to check on you." He says laughing audibly with the playful glint still present in his voice.

"Did you reach there safely?" he asks, now in a more composed voice.

"Yes I did. We are just heading to Maryam's home" I inform.

"So you are still in the car..." he trails.

"Yes..." I answer furrowing my eyebrows at his sentence.

"I was wondering if I could video call you or something. I have been wanting to see you since the time you left" he says nervously.

I should have known.This man!!!

"Adam come on, it has not even been two hours since I have left" I say rolling my eyes.

"It has actually been two hours now and it is indeed enough time for you to be missed habibti." He states in a grumpy voice.

"I'll call back once I reach home alright?" I ask, breathless at the affection in his tone.

How can one love a person so much? I sometimes begin to doubt my own self when he acts so nice. I get so damn overwhelmed with all the love he shows and I desperately pray to Allah to make him feel this special to have me.

"Maira come on... just a few minutes" he asks again.

"I love you Adam" I blurt out feeling my heartbeat speed up.

"Whoa! Okay... I love you more than you can decipher and you know it." he exclaims, an apparent smile in his voice.

Maryam and Alina snicker in the car at my flushed state and I send them a glare which causes them to laugh even more.

"Now back to my request. Can I please call you?" he asks from the phone.

"Technically we are on a call" I state as a matter of fact chuckling to myself.

"Sweetheart, stop playing around and tell me if I can?" he asks again probably rolling his eyes with a cute smile lingering on his face.

Shit I miss him too.

"I am with my friends here in the car"

"I promise I won't talk much and will definitely not look at anything else other than you" he says in such a convincing tone.

Now, how do I deny such a sweet plea? I mean I also am quite eager to see him.

"I'll call you" I state as I hang up on him and call him, a video call now.

"I swear, that husband of yours is adorable" Alina says from behind me.

"He is so damn clingy" Maryam exclaims playfully at the same time.

How can so different souls be best friends?

"He makes me feel extraordinary." I tell them. Maryam glances at me for a second and I am sure she has a soft smile lingering on her face directed towards me while Alina pulls my cheeks saying an 'Aww'.

We walk out of the warm and cozy café where we've been for more than an hour doing nothing but chatting, with our coffee cups and pastries on our table. The café is such a good place to just sit and relax ourselves with the sweet aroma all over the place and the comfortable atmosphere engulfing us.

The day had passed by sooner than I had expected. We had left Maryam's place soon after breakfast and it is already nearing 9 p.m now. Thankfully we had finished with our isha prayers in the small and secluded mosque near the city area and we are planning on heading straight back to Maryam's place.

It is always refreshing to visit Maryam and Alina because of the beautiful place they live in. Surely London city has its own charms but the environment here in Canterbury is amazing and cool. This place might not have as many shops or malls as London to go shopping but just strolling around the streets here is more than enough to clear our heads.

"I am going to pass out as soon as we enter the house" Alina sighs dramatically.

"Dude you were relaxing there in that coffee shop for more that an hour, how can you be still tired?" Maryam asks nudging her with her shoulder.

"I have the art of being tired all the time" Alina says as she flips her hijab.

Maryam groans "How are you even my friend?"

I laugh and so does Alina putting her hands around mine and Maryam's shoulder.

"You are not. Because you guys are my best friends and also my long lost sisters." She says joining us in our laughing selves.

We call a cab and sit into it as my phone starts ringing in my bag.

"Oh wow, I was just now wondering how Adam has not called you in past five whole hours." Maryam says before I could see the caller id. I look at the caller id and indeed it is Adam.

"He really misses her" Alina says teasingly winking her eye.

"Assalamualaikum" I say through the phone once I pick the call up.

"Well at least they send peace to each other everytime they say Salaam when he calls her so many times" Maryam grumbles from beside me before Adam could reply.

"Walaikumassalam, your friends don't like me calling you much, hmm?" He questions chuckling to himself.

"They just don't like being interrupted frequently when we are having our quality time" I clear, a small smile on my face.

"I don't even call that many times" he whines childishly.

"Adam you have called more than a five times today and let us not forget the two video chats we did when I was in the mosque." I say chuckling and rolling my eyes.

"Yeah, Okay. I missed my wife alright" he states grumpily.

"And I am really sorry if I annoyed you by my calls. And I am also truly sorry for irritating your friends" he adds apologetically.

"I appreciate your apology to my friends and I definitely did not get annoyed by your calls." I say smiling heartily.

"But then you missed me too right?" he asks in a smug voice.

"I never said that"

"But lets not forget your calls, you did to check on me" he teases.

"I might have been a bit worried when you didn't reply to my messages or didn't call yourself for a long time." I say, proving my point and turning away from the intimidating gazes of my friends.

"So you sort of missed me" he concludes.

"Yeah maybe" I say rolling my eyes.

"Lying is haraam Maira" he explains as though he is speaking to a kid.

"Okay fine I missed you. Happy now?" I sigh trying to cover up my flushed voice.

"Very happy" he sighs dreamily.

(◍•ᴗ•◍)

I snuggle between Maryam and Alina as I tuck the blanket under my chin.

"Why don't you move here in Canterbury with Adam after your wedding reception?" Maryam proposes the idea.

"It would be wonderful to have you here. Like we can meet anytime we would wish to." Alina exclaims happily over the idea.

"I don't know. We haven't really talked about it yet." I say shrugging under the duvet.

"He also have his job over there, so I don't think so we'll be moving out of the city anytime soon." I add staring at the ceiling.

Alina chuckles suddenly making our heads turn to her. "I wonder what Adam would do if he were to shift out of the country for job purposes" she says smirking coolly.

"He just cannot stay without hearing your voice for a few hours let alone days" Maryam says rolling her eyes.

My heart beat paces up at their words.

"I feel so damn lucky to have him, he makes me feel special. Though I am scared if he doesn't find the same contentment in having me." I say with a sigh.

"I don't even have to tell anything when I am with him, he just gets it without me even having to say it to him. What if I fail to understand him like how he does me?" I think out loud.

"That man loves you Maira, we can feel it in his words." Alina says stressing on her words.

"And with love comes both contentment and understanding" Maryam explains.

I laugh at her philosophical talk. "I never thought that I would hear something like that from you, Maryam." I tease discreetly changing the subject due to my reddening cheeks.

Maryam groans pulling the blanket over her head "I am sleeping now" she exclaims before turning to the other side.

"How is Maryam's other half doing by the way, Maira?" Alina asks trying to pull off Maryam's duvet from her head.

"I am going to push you both off the bed if you don't stop now" she grunts slightly pushing Alina's hand.

"Good night Mrs. Soon to be Usman Abdul Haseeb" Alina giggles putting her hand around the both of us.

"Just shut up already" Maryam grumbles making us both laugh and eventually doze off.

Chapter-16: Missing.

"The world is enjoyment and the best joy in the world is a righteous wife."

[Sahih Muslim 1467]

Assalamualaikum wa rahmatullahi wa barakatuhu

Bismillah

If you haven't offered your salah and it's salah time then please pray and then return, do not delay your prayers.

□♡----------------- ♡□

ADAM

I throw my bag in the back seat of my car and hop in the car to drive back home. College sucks without Maira here. She is the one thing which gets me to get out of the bed in the morning. The thought of seeing her in the college gets me excited to come to college and with her not here, I literally don't feel like starting my day at all.

I am about to start the car when my friend comes knocking on the window "We are going to the bowling place" he says

"And?" I ask eventhough I know what he is implying.

"Come on man, stop sulking around." He says leaning on the car.

"I don't want to come" I speak my thoughts.

"Your wife is going to hate you for becoming such a boredom of a human" he tries to convince.

'You are undeniably plain'

Maira's exaggerated words echoes in my ears, making me smile. Ya Allah I miss her and I miss her so very much.

"Adam hello!!" he snaps his fingers in front of my face.

"Started dreaming of her already?" he asks with an eye roll.

"You are just going to end up missing her even more if you stay alone, come with us" he presses again.

"Alright, what time?" I ask, sighing.

Mama has also been complaining about my sulkiness since the time Maira has left. She'll be happy to not have my brooding self around for some time.

"Evening" he says grinning

"I'll come pick you up." He adds and goes out of my sight.

I exhale deeply and lean my head on the steering wheel. Two days more and then I'll be able to see her with my bare eyes in front of me inshaAllah.

I have called her only once today, in the morning and she had apparently just woken up. I stop myself from calling her again and thank Allah that I did a video call or else I wouldn't have lasted till now.

I desperately hope that I hadn't annoyed her with my calls yesterday and also her friends. I know how much they mean to her. I admit that I had gone a little too overboard with the calls yesterday but how can I help myself when I have got such a wonderful wife.

Alhamdulillah.

I am interrupted again when I start the car, this time because of my phone. I pull it from my pocket and a big smile forms on my face as I look at the caller id.

"Assalamualaikum" I say without wasting a second.

"Walaikumassalam, how are you?" she asks her voice laced with concern.

"I am good and definitely better now that you have called." I say with a smile of contentment.

"Cheesy" she comments.

"You love it" I reply knowing how much she loves these cheesy comments and gestures.

"As though you know me" she scoffs, probably trying to cover her flushed state.

"I've known you enough to know that you're having a crimson shade on your cheeks" I say smirking.

"How was college?" she asks, abruptly changing the subject.

I laugh at her cuteness. Damn I miss this woman so much.

"Can you come a bit earlier?" I ask suddenly feeling her absence around me.

"Why are you answering to my question with a question?" she asks making me chuckle again.

"Because I can" I say childishly.

"What are you doing by the way?" I ask before she could speak.

"We are currently at this beautiful park where I come every time I visit my friends."

"I am glad you are having a good time" I say truly happy for her.

She hums in response before speaking again "What are you doing?"

"Sitting in my car at the college parking lot"

"Okay then. I will talk to you later?" she asks.

"I don't mind continuing the talk though" I say immediately, not liking the idea to stop listening to her voice.

"You cannot stay in the parking lot forever. I'll call you in the evening alright?"

"That reminds me, my friends are asking me to come to the bowling place." I inform.

"That's so cool." She replies excited at the idea.

"Send me the pictures of you bowling. I have always wanted to see you play sports..." she trails off not completing her sentence.

"And?" I ask.

"And nothing. I just want to see you play." she concludes her voice sounding flustered.

"What were you thinking while telling me that-- oh right you have already seen me play sports, haven't you?" I ask now realizing the reason behind her shyness.

"Have I?" she asks rhetorically and a bit breathless.

"Do I need to remind you, sweetheart?" I smirk.

"Adam you really need to go back home and my friends are also probably waiting for me." she says hurriedly hanging up the call causing me to laugh out loudly at her adorable antics.

Oh Allah. I love this woman. I love this woman so damn much.

(◍•ᴗ•◍)

All of us cheer Maxwell, as he strikes all the bowling pins. We have been here for more than two hours. I have successfully sent a couple of pictures of me bowling to Maira and my friends won't stop teasing me about it.

Like I care, I don't mind doing the shittiest things if that's what makes Maira happy.

These people do not know the bliss of having the perfect one who is made especially and particularly for you. I am sure once they get their perfect ones they would act just the same way as I do.

Who would have thought that I would become this person? I crave for her voice, her touch or just a glance from her. I cannot keep my hands to myself when I am with her, my heart races when she gives me that charming smile, it does these somersaults when I hear the sound of her laugh.

The way she knows what I need or the way she understands me without having me to tell it to her is just so overwhelming.

I cannot thank Allah enough for sending her in my life. She has played a major part in making me closer to my Lord. Alhamdulillah.

I hope she feels the same contentment in having me. I am afraid of her not feeling as special to have me as much as I do to have her.

Cheering voices erupt from my friends, breaking my trance. "I guess we are done here, aren't we guys?" Maxwell asks. He has been my best friend from as long as I can remember. That guy knows me in and out. He appreciates the change in me after I have met Maira and he is somewhat jealous of her because according to him I prioritize her more than him.

She is my wife for Allah's sake man.

"Stop day dreaming about your wife, brother. Your smile is attracting women around here." he whispers putting his head around my neck as we walk out of the bowling place.

I glare at him as I look around and indeed there are people looking towards us. Not just women. Tell him to exaggerate things.

(⦿•◡•⦿)

I scroll through my phone debating on calling Maira or not. I have spoken to her just for twice today. I guess this would be okay with her friends, wouldn't it be? Mama and baba roll their eyes as they sit across from me in the living room "Talk to her or just keep that phone away" baba huffs.

"You have been in this state from the past hour" Mama adds.

I huff in exhaustion and keep the phone beside me. "I think she is occupied with other stuff and I don't want to disturb her." I explain

"But I want to talk to her. It has been so many hours that I've heard her voice." I say again.

"You were watching her video just a few minutes back" Mama says slyly.

"Wait! You were watching your wife's videos?" Baba asks cutting off mama.

"Yeah because I was missing her" I exclaim sighing exasperatedly.

"Hey Assalamualaikum everyone" Aisha bounces in the room cheerfully.

"Oh Adam you are still here?" she asks confusedly.

"Yes, why?" I ask furrowing my brows at her bizarre question.

"Because Maira had texted me telling that she has arrived here in London an hour back and I thought that you will be going to see her." she says still with a glint of confusion.

My heart speeds up at the thought of seeing her again as I quickly stand up grabbing my keys from the couch. "Really?" I ask getting stupidly excited.

"Yes of course." She says biting her lips trying to control her laugh.

Then it hits me 'Why would Maira not inform me of her coming back early?' I look up at Aisha to see her on the verge of bursting with laughter and the next thing I hear is her loud laugh erupting from her stupid mouth.

"Your face was priceless" she says through her laughs and I glare at her before chasing her all across the living room and then she runs and locks her bedroom door as soon as she enters it, her laughter still booming inside the house.

I had gotten all excited for just nothing and now I really need to see Maira. So I quickly take my phone out from my pocket and video call her.

And I hate how my heart kicks up a notch at the thought of seeing her although if it is just through a screen.

Stupid heart.

Chapter–17: Preparations.

M AIRA

"I still think that a café would be a better place than a library" Amina whines going towards the furthest part of the library.

"I don't think that we could study in the middle of the crowd in the café for our exams and---" Zainab is cut midway as the librarian shushes us showing a warning glare.

"This is the exact reason of us coming here to study" I whisper, pointing to the librarian as she turns to the corner.

"But we wouldn't even be able to open our mouths here" Amina whisper shouts.

"That is the point Amina, we wouldn't be able to talk and hence, we will all study peacefully without any distractions." Zainab explains

"Alright Miss. Goody two shoes" Amina rolls her eyes as she takes out her books.

I take my books out too and begin to skim over the contents inside. This is the time of the year I dread the most- the examination time.

I just feel worried about not studying anything but I still do not study anything, if that makes any sense. I sigh and shake my head, ready to begin a new topic.

The days have passed rapidly after my little trip to Canterbury and we now have our exams starting early next week. Adam has been busier than me these days considering that these are probably the last set of examinations he will be giving in his life.

I exhale quite audibly, with an oncoming smile on my face at the thought of Adam. He had become extra sweet and cute after I returned from my friends' place. He wouldn't leave my hand when we were together or just always be as near to me as possible.

And I have loved every moment of it. I cannot thank Allah enough for the blessings He has bestowed upon me through Adam.

Two hands suddenly cover my eyes causing me to shriek.

I feel the person lean their head closer to the side of my face as I hear Amina and Zainab's soft giggles.

"Any guesses?" An all too familiar voice whispers in my ear making me smile underneath my niqab.

"Well?" I feign a thoughtful tone in my voice.

"Assalamualaikum sweetheart" he says removing his hands and planting a soft kiss on my cheeks.

"If I could take her with me for a while...?" he trails off asking my friends, flickering his nervous gaze to me.

"I figured that you had stuff to study"

"And why are you here in the first place?" I add trying to raise my eyebrows from under my niqab.

"You texted me a while back telling me that you're headed to the library and yes I have stuff to study but who says that we cannot take a break?" he asks wiggling his eyebrows with a smirk on his face.

I roll my eyes at him and tell my friends that I'll be back in a while, while taking Adam's hand which he had held out.

"I thought we were just going to have a small talk and then get back to studying." I state confusedly as Adam opens his car door for me.

"Come on. A little cup of ice cream wouldn't hurt right?" he winks as he climbs into the driver's seat.

"And I haven't seen you all day" he adds starting the car and moving out of the parking lot.

"How are your preparations going, anyway?" he asks.

"Good but I do not have even a bit of motivation or enthusiasm to keep continuing to study." I say with a deep sigh, placing my legs on the seat and getting comfortable in the coziness of the vehicle.

Adam glances at me with a soft smile for a second before turning back to the road. "How are yours?" I ask now turning my whole body to his side and leaning the side of my head on the head rest.

"We have been having revision sessions at college so it has been quite helpful and productive" he informs nodding his head.

I hum to his answer silently looking over at him. He is in a black jacket with a grey t-shirt underneath it and a light wash jeans paired with it. He has also been wearing the watch that I had given him after the wedding and by the amount of times he has worn that, I wouldn't be surprised to see it getting worn out a bit too quickly.

"It is not fair how you can check me out all you want and I don't even get to see your face" Adam whines throwing a pouty glance at me.

I just chuckle at his childishness and feel a little droopiness seeping in.

(◍•ᴗ•◍)

I wake up to a mellifluous voice calling my name and gentle strokes on the back of my palm "You will have to drink a milkshake rather than eating an ice-cream if you do not wake up now" Adam whispers as I begin to open my eyes and rub the sleep off them.

"You should have woken me up earlier" I say sitting up straighter.

He smiles gazing at me without speaking anything for a while. "What?" I ask suddenly becoming self-conscious and realizing that my niqab was still on.

He shakes his head with the smile still present on his face "Your voice is amazing when you wake up" he says.

I chuckle at his response "It is usually the other way round, the girl would like the hoarse voice of the guy when he wakes up." I say as I take my ice-cream cup from him.

Cookies 'n' cream with extra toppings.

"Then I will wait till you hear my just woken up voice to get that compliment from you" he says smirking.

I roll my eyes and lower my niqab to finally devour the ice-cream "Why did you not remove my niqab?" I ask suddenly remembering.

He throws a nervous glance "I just was not completely sure that you would be ok with it" he says. "Wouldn't it feel a bit creepy or uncomfortable?" he asks.

"Of course not Adam" I exclaim shaking my head. "You are my husband Alhamdulillah and I would never feel creepy or uncomfortable if you would remove my niqab. I trust you" I concluded with a sigh in a serious tone and a goofy smile appears on his stupidly pretty face.

How could a person smile so beautifully when there is a serious conversation on-going?

"Stop smiling" I order, pointing my index at him.

"Well how can I, when you so sweetly declared me as your husband?" he asks cheekily. "And lets not forget the way you called out my name" he adds nodding to himself.

"You just got that out of the whole lot of my little speech?' I ask incredulously.

He laughs quietly and leans in to peck my cheeks "I got it sweetheart, I know you trust me and all but it was just my thought. Wouldn't happen next time alright?" he assures. I nod at him and smile again looking at my ice-cream "Thanks for the ice-cream, it's my favorite and that too with extra toppings" I grin taking a spoonful of it in my mouth.

He hums silently and says a quiet 'I know' before bringing a spoonful of his ice-cream near my mouth "Taste it" he insists.

I eat it and offer my cup for him to taste. "You should return back soon" I remind him "A break doesn't mean to get off for the whole day" I tease, smiling slyly at him.

"I was just thinking of dropping it today and making a fresh start tomorrow" he says looking down at his cup and then at me.

I roll my eyes "You didn't even have enough time to study yesterday and now not even today" I sigh. "I am just afraid that I would become the reason of you not doing well in your exams" I continue seriously, voicing out my thoughts.

"I guess we should keep our meetings to a minimum until the end of our exams" I add.

"What!? Absolutely not!" he exclaims in a higher voice.

"You don't have to be worried about me not doing well and especially not because of you. Because if anything, you are my extra motivation to do better" he says with a wink.

"How cheesy is that now?" I feign a grimace having the last spoon of the ice-cream and throwing the cup in the thrash.

"You love it, don't you?" he asks smirking and throwing his cup away too.

"I'll have to think about that answer now.." I trail biting my lower lip to control my laugh when he narrows his eyes at me.

"There is no choice. You will have to love it and tolerate it" he says with the same look and then smiles widely before continuing "Because Mrs. Maira Abdul Haseeb you are stuck with this person even for the hereafter" he says tapping my nose with his index finger.

His smiles are literally the best-- no actually the worst thing in the world because my heart just takes up the fastest pace when he smiles.

I laugh heartily, shaking my head at his words.

This boy can never fail to make me fall for him all over again

Chapter-18: Celebration.

MAIRA

"Such a bliss to know that exams are over and semester break is starting tomorrow" Zainab says with a dramatic sigh as we climb onto the brick railing and sit facing the ground area, where the guys are practicing for their game this Friday.

"What are your plans for the holidays?" Amina asks.

"I don't particularly have any yet" Zainab informs and then both of them look towards me.

I roll my eyes at them "As if you both don't already know"

"Oh right!" they both nod in realization. "And you guys are coming no matter what" I declare.

"Of course we will inshAllah" they both say in unison.

"Careful" someone calls out from the field as a ball comes flying towards Amina. I pull Amina to the right as she thankfully dodges the ball. "Who even thought that I was the damn goalpost?" she exclaims incredulously.

Zainab snickers "It's alright. You weren't going to die or anything"

Amina narrows her eyes at her "You weren't going to die or anything" she mocks Zainab. "Wait till the ball hits you" she adds, huffing childishly.

Zainab scoffs and faces to the field "And here comes your prince charming" she exclaims winking at me.

"Assalamualaikum" Adam says coming to where we are sitting. "Walaikumassalam, how have you been?" I ask as he places his hands on the either sides of me on the railings. "Better now" he says cheekily. I chuckle "Good that the exams are done, right?" I ask.

He sighs "Yup very good but this practice just after those hectic exams is seriously not good"

"Don't worry you're all free after the game, so just bare it, I guess?" I suck at cheering people up.

I grimace at my own words "Sorry that was meant to make you feel better" I say and Adam chuckles "Just the thought of you makes me feel better" he teases "But on a second thought, a dinner date tonight would definitely be nice" he adds expectantly.

I sigh slowly "I am actually going out with my friends today" I say in a low voice pointing to Amina and Zainab who are completely engrossed in their own conversations. Adam groans and lowers his head on my lap "Please?" he persuades.

"You could still come over early for breakfast tomorrow" I say in a convincing tone. "And it will be just today, we all will probably not meet until our walima" I add before continuing "You can relax today back at home"

He hums with his head still lowered "And you are all sweaty and gross and I would very much like if you would pick your head up" I say teasingly. He shakes his head more ruffling my abaya, chuckling to himself. "I am going to make you wash this abaya of mine" I say feigning a serious tone.

He lifts his head up and gazes at me "I love you" he says suddenly and stands on his toes to kiss my niqab clad forehead. I grin down at him "It is relieving to not have to look up at you" I say and he raises his brows "I thought you liked being a shorty" he says with a hint of tease in his voice.

I roll my eyes at him "Firstly, I am not as short as you are making me sound and second, I still like being shorter than you is what I had said earlier" I explain. "And I like this position of ours, that's it" I say pointing my finger at us.

He laughs softly at my explanation causing me to scowl "You can't always just laugh when I am here basically explaining stuff to you" he chuckles gain. The nerve of this guy. "I just find it amusing when you go on explaining such a simple thing and it makes you look more beautiful than you already are and then I end up thinking of how blessed I am to have you amidst the billion more people in the world" he concludes.

I am at loss of words at his words. He definitely has the most beautiful way of choosing his words when he speaks-at least to me.

"And I so much wish for this conversation to happen when we are not in the field of our college" he adds and my eyes snap up to look at the people around us and I glance at Amina and Zainab to see that they are now sitting at the far end of the railing and not where they previously there. Just when did they go there?

"I think that I have to get going now" I say looking back at Adam who is still in the same position. He sighs longingly as I smile at the man whom I have come to love, enormously.

"And I love you Adam, though I might not be able to express it as nicely as you always do but you have to know and trust me that I love you with my whole heart and whenever you say things like you said just now, my love for you grows even more and I would never want it any other way" I tell him softly with a smile which I don't know if he is able to sense.

He looks at me with an unwavering gaze and I begin to recollect my words to make sure that I didn't say anything wrong.

"You have no idea how I feel listening to you say it out loud even though I've known that it was there in your heart before and you say that you are not able to express it nicely" he says shaking his head. "Though I would very much like to see your face before you leave, I can live with the sparkle I see in your eyes now, when you smile" he says before planting a kiss on my forehead and letting me go to my friends.

(⫴•‿•⫴)

We go around The Body Shop, randomly picking up some tryout lotions and perfumes and then moving on to the next ones. "I am actually going to buy this lotion" Zainab says smelling the lotion again. "I cannot get enough of this fragrance" she continues to smell it.

"Okay then let us get out of here" Amina exclaims hooking her hands with us and moving towards the cashier.

We stroll around almost all the shops in the mall till our stomachs rumble out due to lack of food. We go to a small café just a block away from the mall gushing over the kids that go along with their parents and over the loving couples who laugh and smile at one another "The world is making me feel so damn single today" Amina says dramatically.

"Just look around and you might actually find the one for you" Zainab whispers playfully "Oh please. I just want Allah to send my soul mate to me as soon as possible" Amina says, sighing dreamily. "Yeah right. These nikahs happening all around is just overwhelming" Zainab agrees.

Well, I don't think so I would have any say in this.

We have some satisfying and good food at the café before calling it a day and heading to our houses. Me and Zainab are going back together since her home is just on the way for me.

"Today was indeed a good day, wasn't it?" Zainab asks as we get closer to her house. "It was Alhamdulillah and I really hope to seeing you guys sooner" I say glancing at her and then looking back at the road.

"I do too inshaAllah" she says as I stop near the gate of her house.

"Ma'salaam" she says giving me a hug and going in her house.

I reach my house and park the car to see Usman's car already present there. He is very rarely back this early. I ring the bell and Usman himself comes to open the door. I raise my eyebrows at him "You are early today?" I ask getting in. "Assalamualaikum" he says rolling his eyes. Well ok, no witty reply?

I furrow my eyebrows as I see both mama and baba in the living room having some sort of conversation. "Assalamualaikum" I exclaim going further in and giving mama and baba light hugs.

"What's up?" I ask sitting down on the couch, removing my niqab and looking at them.

"Usman had something to tell us about" Baba informs looking at me and then at Usman.

I nod urging them to continue whatever it was as I feel my heart rate picking up. "I have been wanting to tell you about this for a long time now" Usman starts.

I look at mama and baba to see a knowing look on their faces. So they already know I guess. "I have been interested in a person and wanted mama and baba to go with a proposal to her place" he says looking at me and then lowering his eyes.

I look at mama and baba to see a smile lingering on their faces. "You guys already know who it is, don't you?" I ask narrowing my eyes at them.

Baba chuckles "First listen to your brother's confession. He will ball his eyes out if he doesn't get to tell it to you" he says motioning towards Usman causing me to laugh at Usman's annoyed face.

"Okay sorry go ahead" I tell him and he again gets that serious and nervous expression on his face "It's...it is Maryam" he says in a rushed voice before closing his eyes tight.

"I knew it" I exclaim loudly before leaping on him for a tight hug. "You are not supposed to say that out loud" he mutters in my ear just so I could hear. "Oops" I stick my tongue out.

"I mean that I was...uhm I am actually very happy" I stutter "My brother and my best friend" I say with a happy sigh.

"How could you be so sure that it is your friend Maryam? I mean there are so many other Maryams in the world" mama asks and I glance at Usman with a knowing look.

"That is just the first person that came to my mind" I shrug hoping to sound convincing. "So about the proposal?" baba begins "When do you think that we should go?" he asks.

"I think it would be better if we do this as soon as possible." I tell and Usman smirks at me.

You owe me dear brother.

Mama and baba talk about it further and then concludes saying that we can finalize the date tomorrow. Usman rushes to his room as soon as the conversation ends and I go after him. "Oh come on. Open the damn door" I call out as Usman hurriedly closes the door before I reach it.

"I would never do the mistake of letting you tease me the whole night and listening to your 'I knew it's and 'I told you's" he says from inside.

"But I actually did tell you and I want to know how you finally realized your true feelings and undying love for my best friend" I say grinning.

"This is the one reason I wouldn't dare to open the door. Go Maira, go to your room and stop bothering me" he says loudly.

"Fine I am going" I call out "I anyway can't wait to tell Alina and Maryam" I say teasingly and just then the door opens as Usman storms out of the door glaring hard at me. I laugh seeing his scowling face "Don't you dare tell her about any of this before we go to her place" he warns "And if I do?" I grin widely. "I will take all the snacks that you have stocked up in cupboard of the stairs" he smirks and my smile falters a bit.

"How the hell do you know my little hideout?" I ask flabbergasted. No one except me and myself knows about this. At least untill now.

"I can hear when you sneak out of your room in the middle of the night, stupid" he says rolling his eyes. "And my room is just right next to yours so it's not a surprise that I have seen you go there and take snacks from the cupboard" he adds.

"How did you even get the ridiculous idea of keeping your eatables there?" he asks shaking his head and leaning on the wall beside him, folding his arms on his chest.

"Well, what can I say? I am just a genius like that" I smirk. "Sure" he says sarcastically before going towards his room again. "Hey you still didn't tell me about your moment of realization of your feelings towards Maryam" I tease again.

"You are surely not going to find that snacks there anymore" he huffs. "You do that and Maryam will know every detail of your little confession earlier" I state grinning as I walk towards my room.

"And we are surely having a celebration tomorrow of your confession" I say loudly before I hear him shut his bedroom door, grumbling about how I manage to annoy him all the time.

What are sisters are for then?

Chapter-19: New Favorite.

M AIRA

I never thought that come over early for breakfast meant to come early and ruin my beauty sleep and that to on the first morning of my holidays. Adam was literally here at 8 a.m, who even wakes up so early on a holiday?

Lucky for him, my parents were awake and he was with them for half an hour and then he came up here to my room to wake me up from my sleep at 8:30 a.m. Who even does that? After an hour of continuous persuasion and coaxing, here I am grumbling at my lack of sleep and brushing my teeth at the same time, while the cruel and absolute meanie is lying peacefully on the bed outside.

"I can hear you whining from out here sweetheart" Adam calls out from my bedroom, chuckling.

"It is meant for you to be heard" I call back wiping my mouth with the towel and stepping out of the bathroom to see him still in the same position as before. He lifts his head from the pillow to grin at me before plopping his head back on the pillow.

I narrow my eyes at him even though he is not seeing and stomp my way to the dresser. He better make this early waking up worth it.

"It is actually cute seeing you all fired up" he says smiling and sitting up on the bed. I roll my eyes at him through the mirror.

"So you are not speaking to me now?" he asks amusedly raising his eyebrows. I stay silent, biting my inner cheek to stop myself from smiling.

"Oh come on" he trails off as he stands up and comes towards me. I finish tying my hijab and move away from the dresser before he could reach me.

"Zawjati" he tries again as I put on a long cardigan over my top and go to open the door all the while stopping myself from laughing at his scowling figure.

He is the one who looks cute doing all this.

He holds my wrist, stopping me from opening the door and turns me around to face him. "Talk to me" he says looking directly in my eyes.

He tilts his head cutely when I don't make any effort to speak to him. "I am sorry for annoying you and waking you up early on a holiday, but you were the one who said that we'll meet early at breakfast today"

"But this early" I groan.

"It's because I had made plans for breakfast for only the two of us today but somebody wouldn't get up from their bed and I had to postpone it for lunch" he says with a single shouldered shrug.

"I am sorry that you had to cancel it out because of me" I say sighing, suddenly feeling guilty.

"It is completely alright and I didn't actually cancel it out, it's just postponed. We'll get to have breakfast with your family" he says smiling and caressing the back of my palm with the pad of his thumb.

I smile back at him turning to open the door "Baba was talking about Usman to me before I came up here" he says coming out with me and holding my hand.

"I am so damn excited to see Maryam's reaction to this" I say excitedly.

"I've been telling her forever about Usman's feeling towards her" I continue.

He nods smiling "When are you guys going to go to their place?" he asks climbing down the stairs. "Baba said that we would discuss it today, we didn't have any family discussions after I talked to you on phone yesterday" I say looking up at him.

We walk in the living room to see baba scrolling through his phone and mama probably in the kitchen. He looks up at me and Adam and raises his eyebrows "Up early today?" he asks with a knowing look.

"Please don't remind her again baba" Adam says chuckling and goes to sit with him on the couch. I go along with him as he is still holding my hand. I take my hand out of his as he sits across baba "I had to deal with a grumpy Maira for thirty minutes straight only for waking her up early" he adds winking at me. Baba laughs at his words and I glare playfully at him "You are supposed to be not laughing at this baba" I state and he laughs even more heartily.

"I'm going to deal with you two later" I say pointing my index finger at them and going towards the kitchen.

"Hey what did I do?" Adam asks loudly as I chuckle my way to mama.

"I don't even know how that boy handles you" mama says shaking her head and I narrow my eyes at her.

"There is nothing much to handle about me" I tell with my eyes still narrowed.

"And you guys are supposed to be on my side" I add scoffing and climbing on the kitchen bar stool.

"There are no sides anymore between you both honey" she says smiling at me. I smile back at her and nod "Usman is not up yet?" I ask. "He was up till late I guess, I heard him walking to the kitchen in the middle of the night" mama says furrowing her brows.

"I am sure his excitement kept him awake" I say smirking. "Oh stop troubling him, he was on the verge of crying yesterday in front of us" she says laughing.

"I know right, he was acting like a kid who got his favorite toy stolen when I teased him last night" I laugh recalling his face.

"How mean of you guys!" Usman exclaims coming behind me and hitting my head. "Oww, all I did was say the truth" I say rubbing the spot he hit.

"All I did was say the truth" he mocks before sitting on the stool beside mine. "Why is your prince charming here this early anyway?" he asks wiggling his eyebrows.

"He had made plans for breakfast" I inform pouring the juice in the jug.

"Then why are you still here?" he asks raising his eyebrows.

"He postponed it to lunch 'cause I didn't wake up early" I shrug.

"Such a spoil sport" he rolls his eyes.

"Such a spoil sport" I mock him back.

"And I was acting like a kid" he says.

"And I was acting like a kid" I mock again smiling slyly at him.

"I will push you off the chair if you don't stop right now" he glares pointing his index finger at me.

"I will push you off the chair if you don't stop right now" I continue smirking.

"Mama you shouldn't yell at me if she falls" he warns giving me a side glance.

"Mama you shouldn't yell--" I begin to mock again as mama cuts me off.

"You both are not getting any breakfast if you don't quit acting like children" Mama warns.

Me and Usman look at each other and bite back our laughs looking at mama's angry face. "You have your husband sitting in the living room and you are probably going get married by the end of this year and you guys still behave as little kids" mama says huffing, pointing her cooking spoon at the both of us.

Usman mutters a silent 'inshAllah' when mama says about his marriage and I roll my eyes. I smile sheepishly looking up at mama and stand up to arrange the table.

All of us come up at the dining table and Adam glances up at me and then looks back down at the table. I go into the kitchen to grab another plate and Adam follows behind discreetly trying to wash his hands.

I look up at him to see him already looking back at me. I raise my eyebrows at him questioning him silently at his behavior "What?" he asks with the littlest smile. "I am just making sure that you are ok now" he says with a shrug.

I roll my eyes smiling at him "And you most definitely are" he adds coming near me and caressing my cheeks. "Am I?" I ask playfully.

He nods "Yes, with the smile that is lingering here you are absolutely alright" he whispers with a wider smile.

"Let us go out there before we are being called" I tell, dragging him to the dining area.

(◍•ᴗ•◍)

"You are just over analyzing things Adam" I say sighing and leaning on the window of his car.

"I am not" he says sternly.

"I could see him literally eyeing you like a bloody pervert" he says gritting his teeth and clenching tighter around the steering wheel.

"Relax there buddy" I chuckle, patting his shoulder. "And even if he was looking, there is nothing for him to look at, at all" I say with a shrug.

He sighs as he glances at me and brings his hand to hold mine on my lap "You don't understand sweetheart" he begins as he interlocks our fingers "Just hearing your voice makes my heartbeat race, so you think I don't know what it feels to look at you even if you're covered" he states tilting his head to look at me, his face a bit softened from before. "I should have just punched him in the face to make him understand to not look at something which is not his'" he grumbles tightening his hold on my hand.

I chuckle at his rant as we turn to the street of my house. "Thankfully this happened by the end of out little outing or else it would have been ruined badly" I say turning to look at his face "And it is really cute to see you all fired up" I tease quoting his words from morning and he scoffs with a hint of smile on his face.

The place where Adam had planned the lunch was beautiful, it was a lookout restaurant with a lake view on the side of the restaurant and the best thing about it was the tinted glass wall where nothing could be seen from the outside and we could also enjoy the lake view in our private booths.

The restaurant was in the outskirts of the city and it had taken us a while to reach there so we strolled around the place until isha prayer and then had our dinner from another wonderful diner and left to get back home. It was a wonderful and relaxing day to start off our semester break Alhamdulillah.

"I would have seriously liked it if you could've come home with me" he says turning in the driveway of my place.

"It is already late now but I am telling you that I will come tomorrow or the day after" I say fixing my niqab to get down the car.

"Let just cut that to tomorrow, no day after" he says turning the car off. "I will try to inshaAllah but no promises" I wink as I unlock the door and move out of his car.

"See you love, Ma'salaam" I add.

"Hey wait!" he calls getting out of the car. I furrow my eyebrows as he comes to my side quickly and wraps his arms around my waist "What?" I ask confusedly.

He grins down at me "You cannot say stuff like that and just leave" he whispers leaning his forehead on mine. "What stuff exactly?" I ask again.

He sighs "Ma'salaam my love" he says still not leaving me and I realize what he was taking about. I smile looking down from him and silently thanking Allah for the niqab to cover my probably deep-red cheeks.

"This is my new favorite thing which you say" he says chuckling.

"What was it before?" I ask looking at him.

"My name when you say it" he smirks and I inhale nervously.

"Bye! Now seriously" I say trying to get away from him.

"I love you sweetheart" he says with such intensity that it makes me almost breathless.

"I love you more, now bye" I say removing his hand from my waist.

"Just bye?" he asks tilting his head and holding my wrist.

"Oh Allah! You are just so crazy Adam" I laugh taking my hand out of his and going to the door.

How does one deal with so damn much of love and affection? This thought almost makes me tear up. Do I even deserve all this?

Alhamdulillah My Rabb.

I hear him laughing loudly before I ring the bell. Usman comes to open the door and I remove my niqab and look back at Adam who is now leaning on his car and waves at me.

I wave back and get inside the house to see Usman's grim face "That sickening smile says it all" he mumbles before going further in. I laugh at him shaking my head unable to remove the smile off my face. I turn back to look at Adam who winks at me before going to his car door and getting in.

My love.

Chapter–20: Verdict.

MAIRA

"I am going to stab myself with this fork with all the weddings happening around me." Alina grumbles chewing down the piece of cake and setting aside the plate.

"Ya Allah just get me married to someone already." she exclaims plopping back on the bed.

"And you traitor" she says suddenly pointing at me.

I raise my eyebrows at her "You couldn't have even bothered to inform me about all of this before?" she says narrowing her eyes.

"And trust you to not blabber it out to Maryam?" I ask knowingly.

"I wouldn't have" she mumbles quietly after a moment.

"You know you would have done it and Usman had anyway wanted it to be a surprise for her" I say nodding towards Maryam who was currently dealing with mixed emotions.

"He is just so sweet, isn't he?" Alina asks nudging Maryam.

Maryam scowls back at Alina and turns to me "A little heads up wouldn't have hurt anyone." she says sighing.

"I have been going on and on about both of you for an eternity and you both seem to always deny me, so deal with it now" I say with a shrug.

"But anyway what is your final verdict?" Alina asks cocking her head at Maryam.

"Are you Maryam Khan ready to take Usman Abdul Haseeb as your husband for an eternity and everything after it?" she continues in a deep voice.

"Shut up already" Maryam huffs and fixes her already fixed hijab.

I sigh and rub her arm "There is nothing to actually be so nervous about, I mean I know that you cannot actually stop the nervousness but knowing that it is just Usman should calm you a bit down" I say comfortingly.

"That is the exact thing which spikes my nervousness" Maryam counters.

"So you are ok with someone else coming up at your home with a proposal for you?" Alina asks smirking and wiggling her brows.

"I didn't m--" Maryam is cut short in her words as her mom comes in knocking on the door.

"Usman is waiting for you in the lawn if you're ready." She says quietly. Maryam inhales sharply and nods, telling her that she'll be out in a moment.

"You are chaperoning us right?" Maryam asks nervously.

"I am and don't worry I will be there to sneak you out if you don't want to be there any longer and to keep my brother in check" I joke trying to light her a bit.

"Thanks" she exhales softly and hugs me.

"Hey you cannot just leave me out here" Alina says hugging us both, causing us to chuckle.

(◍•ᴗ•◍)

"You should actually be thanking me for her acceptance of this proposal" I say as I lean on Usman's door frame.

"And why is that?" he asks lifting his head from his laptop.

"You wouldn't have been this delighted if it wasn't for my coaxing." I say smiling slyly.

"Oh please. It is just my charm that she couldn't resist." he says smugly.

"I would actually be on a call with Maryam and hiding the phone behind me for all you know?" I say raising my eyebrows. A look of pure panic crosses his face before he stables himself. "You would not." He states rather nervously.

"It's a good thing that I actually like the both of you or else I wouldn't have any second thoughts in doing that." I laugh and turn back to my room as he scoffs.

It has been two days since we've arrived from Maryam's place and we got a call this morning from her father giving us a positive response for the proposal. Alhamdulillah, Usman is literally flying up above in the sky after hearing their response.

I plop down on the bed picking my phone to call Adam. It has been two whole days that I have seen him in person and I actually miss him, though we have our frequent calls and video chats. A soft knock on the door causes me to look up from my phone.

The door opens slowly before I could respond and after a brief pause Adam pokes his head from the door. I raise my eyebrows not able to bite down the wide smile appearing on my face. My heartbeat kicks up a notch seeing him for real just when I was missing him and I rise from my bed to embrace him as he now fully comes inside the room.

"I have missed you." I say sighing contently in his arms. He exhales softly as he kisses the top of my head "I've missed you more and Assalamualaikum."

"Walaikumassalam" I mumble against his chest not willing to let go of him. "Wouldn't you ask why or how I came this late?" he asks rubbing my back benignly.

"I'm just grateful that you are here" I say, shaking my head.

"No questions asked?" he asks, a smile present in his voice. "No questions asked." I state firmly.

"I am starting to love this self of yours" he says and I look up at him, a soft smile on my face. He kisses my forehead and leads us to the bed.

"So..." he trails off rubbing his hands together, sitting on the bed facing towards me. I raise my eyebrows at his excited state and nod my head urging him to continue.

"I have officially got a job in the company" he exclaims with a wide grin.

"MashaAllah, congrats bro" I bump my shoulder to his and wiggle my brows. His face forms into a scowl and he nudges me away "Not bro okay" he warns and I stifle my laugh.

"Dude?" I try.

"Better" he hums.

"Anyway, did you tell the others? I am sure your mother would've been more that happy to hear that."

"She was, I came here just after I informed her, she was ecstatic" he says with an apparent smile.

"Well...when is the celebration?"

"Whenever you'd want to, we can go get some ice cream right now if you wish" he suggests rolling the sleeves of his grey shirt.

"If you are the one to tell mama and baba" I bargain.

He sighs biting his lip "Done, you go get ready and I will ask your parents to take their daughter to an ice cream date"

(⑩•‿•⑩)

"Now, now am I seeing two colorful cups of ice creams in The Adam Abdullah's hand?" I ask grinning ear to ear and wiggling in my seat.

"You are rubbing off on me" he says narrowing his eyes but with a hint of smile on his face.

"Your life is getting a fill of colors with the help of this ice cream" I joke.

"Indeed" he says handing me my cup with the sweetest smile.

"I am getting used to this sweet smile of yours, y' know" I say, taking a bit of my ice cream.

"I wonder if you too feel the same way about my face or me in all because I tend to bore people out very soon." I say with a one-shouldered shrug.

"It's a wonder in itself that you haven't already left" I add, shifting my gaze to the tilted head of Adam.

He exhales audibly and shakes his head slightly.

"You've got a very much wrong idea in your head sweetheart, I am getting used to you and all your little things in such a high speed that it might even be unhealthy" he continues.

"You could never bore me out, not now, not ever, if anything, I would only feel that I am not getting enough of you even after spending every damn moment with you"

"And I would never be able to leave you" he continues with a light chuckle "I couldn't think of it even in my head"

And I think that I would pass out due to the effect of his words on my heart.